"I think we can ~~try again,~~ Anna said as she stepped under the outdoor shower head and pulled the chain.

"Do you?" Mitch asked, taking the chain out of her hand and holding it for her. Water splashed on his jeans and one sandy, bare foot rested in a growing puddle while the other was propped against the wall, his body totally relaxed.

Anna didn't reply. Instead, she closed her eyes and turned her face up into the spray, stretching her arms above her head to wash her hair. Suddenly a warm mouth was covering hers and the heated feeling she'd noticed before turned into a full-scale meltdown.

The water kept coming and so did his kiss— warm, delicious, insistent, caressing her lips and turning her inside out. Her arms dropped to his shoulders in slow motion as he began to kiss the corners of her mouth ever so slowly, savoring every touch.

Anna was drowning in water and desire, both of them running down her body in lazy, undulating waves, washing away her resistance. . . .

WHAT ARE *LOVESWEPT* ROMANCES?

They are stories of true romance and touching emotion. We believe those two very important ingredients are constants in our highly sensual and very believable stories in the *LOVESWEPT* line. Our goal is to give you, the reader, stories of consistently high quality that may sometimes make you laugh, sometimes make you cry, but are always fresh and creative and contain many delightful surprises within their pages.

Most romance fans read an enormous number of books. Those they truly love, they keep. Others may be traded with friends and soon forgotten. We hope that each *LOVESWEPT* romance will be a treasure—a "keeper." We will always try to publish

LOVE STORIES YOU'LL NEVER FORGET
BY AUTHORS YOU'LL ALWAYS REMEMBER

The Editors

LOVESWEPT® • 198

Glenna McReynolds
Scout's Honor

BANTAM BOOKS
TORONTO • NEW YORK • LONDON • SYDNEY • AUCKLAND

For my special friend,
Rebecca

SCOUT'S HONOR

A Bantam Book / July 1987

LOVESWEPT® *and the wave device are registered*
trademarks of Bantam Books, Inc. Registered in U.S. Patent
and Trademark Office and elsewhere.

If you would be interested in receiving protective vinyl
covers for your Loveswept books, please write to this address
for information:

Loveswept
Bantam Books
P.O. Box 985
Hicksville, NY 11802

ISBN 0-553-21834-4

Published simultaneously in the United States and Canada

Bantam Books are published by Bantam Books, Inc. Its trade-
mark, consisting of the words "Bantam Books" and the por-
trayal of a rooster, is Registered in U.S. Patent and Trademark
Office and in other countries. Marca Registrada. Bantam
Books, Inc., 666 Fifth Avenue, New York, New York 10103.

PRINTED IN THE UNITED STATES OF AMERICA

O   0 9 8 7 6 5 4 3 2 1

One

Anna Lange sat at the bar and let her gaze roam over the lush interior of Runner's Cay Casino. She checked the room for familiar faces, but found few, because Nassau's season didn't start until December and December was two months away. Her chances of getting together a private poker game for the weekend were looking slim.

"Your drink, Ms. Lange," the bartender said, delivering a crystal flute of champagne.

"Thank you," Anna said with a smile. She pulled a five-dollar chip out of her beaded clutch bag and laid it on the bar for a tip. "What time is it?"

"Eight-thirty, ma'am."

"Thank you." She was right on time. St. John should be here.

Anna picked up her glass and turned back to the casino, this time ignoring the gamblers and looking for one special face. She didn't know the stranger's name, but she had a feeling he knew hers.

She'd first noticed the man two nights ago in San Francisco. It would have been hard not to notice someone who was watching you with such unconcealed intensity. Especially when that someone stood out like an innocent abroad amidst the international clientele of Mr. Wong's private gambling club. The stranger had kept his distance, smiling each time he caught her eye but never approaching her. She had assumed he was a shy pursuer of her affections and, surprisingly, had found herself wishing he had more courage.

When he failed to introduce himself she had dismissed him, until he'd shown up last night on the opposite side of the Runner's Cay baccarat table, over three thousand miles from where she'd seen him the night before. Within minutes of watching him play she had known he wasn't a gambler. He seemed more interested in smiling at her than watching his cards. Anna played the odds—that was her life—and she would have taken all bets against his arrival in Nassau being a coincidence.

Rather than being unnerved by the man following her, she had methodically run down a list of possible reasons of why he would do so. An admirer would have approached her in San Francisco. She didn't believe her father would have stooped so low as to have her followed by a private detective, although she couldn't completely discount the idea. That left the most logical conclusion: He was a reporter looking to dig up old gossip.

Anna sipped her champagne and searched the casino again. A slow smile curved her lips as she spotted her stranger walking toward her. She had wondered how long it would take for him to get his courage up.

Dusk had stolen over the Bahamian island like a soft rainbow of muted color. It backlighted the lanky masculine figure, but she knew it was he. If he was a reporter, he was in for the coldest shoulder he'd ever gotten. All she wanted was his name. St. John would check him out and then she'd get to the bottom of his game.

"San Francisco get too hot to handle?" she asked as he neared her, acknowledging his approach by taking the advantage of the opening gambit. Her subtle allusion to the illegality of their Chinatown game was another move calculated to put him in his place.

"It was hot for a while," he admitted, grinning crookedly, "but there was a noticeable cooling after you left. Do you always clean a place out, Ms. Lange?" His easily placed western drawl confirmed her guess about his nationality—American.

"Whenever possible, Mr. . . . ?" She caught his gaze and felt a moment's surprise. She hadn't known anyone could have eyes that soft, or that richly brown. They weren't a gambler's eyes.

"Summers. Mitch Summers." He moved in closer and rested his elbow on the bar, then picked up her hand and lifted it to his lips. He softly brushed his mouth across her knuckles and sapphire ring while smiling into her eyes.

The only thing unusual about his action was her response. The fact that she even had one caught her off guard. In the split second it took her to register this new twist, he turned her hand over and kissed her palm. His breath warmed her skin, and the heat seemed to race up her arm, bringing a flush to her cheeks.

She snatched her hand back, her eyes widening in an unaccustomed loss of composure at his schoolboy ploy. She made no pretense of avoiding his gaze, and actively looked for an escape route away from the suddenly too-cozy corner of the bar. Where was St. John?

She decided to try the direct approach, hoping he'd step back far enough so that she wouldn't have to push by him. "Excuse me, Mr. Summers. I have an appointment to keep." The cool look she lowered at him was completely wasted, though. All his attention was focused on the décolletage of her gown.

She couldn't blame him. The dress was designed to distract, its midnight-blue folds of shirred satin molded to her figure like a second skin, the neckline cut to reveal. But most people who traveled in her circle would hardly look twice. Mitch Summers was on his fourth or fifth look by now. She saw the question in his eyes—"What holds it up?"—and she wasn't about to satisfy his gauche curiosity.

"Excuse me," she said with more force, reaching out to push him aside lightly. Her hand encountered a wall of resistance, a rock-hard chest that mere politeness wouldn't budge. The time for pleasantries had ended.

"Mr. Summers." She paused and took a deep breath, inadvertently increasing his fascination with her breasts. "You have a choice. You can either step aside and let me pass . . . or I can break your face." She spoke very quietly, one winged brow arched above her eye.

A slow, impish grin spread across his face as he considered her words and let his gaze roam from her cleavage up to her face.

"That's a tough one, Miss Lange. Exactly how badly are you going to hurt me?"

"Badly enough," she replied. He was teasing her, and she had to fight back a smile at his audacity. Suave and debonair he was not.

"Could we talk about it over dinner?"

"No. Thank you."

There was no reason to continue the conversation now that she knew his name, but still she was becoming mildly intrigued. He was out of his class, whether he realized it or not. She'd noticed that at the baccarat table. He'd kept to the minimum bet and played like a novice. Baccarat wasn't a game of judgment or skill, but most people played it with a finesse he had lacked.

But he was cute. Cute? A puzzled frown flashed across her face as she took another look at him. She hadn't described anyone as cute since she was sixteen. Must be his eyes, she thought. They looked so guileless, so warm and inviting. Definitely not the blank coldness she was used to encountering in the casinos. Or maybe it was his face. He had a face that hid the years, lean and outdoorsy, with a grin that went one way while his nose tried not to go the other. His nose had been broken, and she couldn't help but wonder how. He didn't look like a fighter. He also didn't look like a private detective. He lacked the worn-out, world-weary countenance of a man who had seen too much of the seedy side of life.

Still, there was something special in his face and the way he held his body, something Anna instinctively recognized: confidence, easy and masculine. She had faced false confidence many times across a poker table, and she knew the real thing when she saw it. This man knew who he was, knew he didn't belong here, and couldn't have cared less.

Another smile flirted with her mouth. Mitch Summers *was* intriguing, but she had all the information she needed. She geared herself up for another, firmer brush-off, but before the words were out of her mouth she felt a clammy hand slide up the the bare skin of her back. In an instant she checked Mitch—one hand around a highball glass, the other shoved in a pocket—and her head snapped around.

"Hi, sweetheart," Larry Walters, pit boss of Runner's Cay, drawled in her ear. "Glad to see you haven't forgotten us." Her skin crawled where he touched her, and she flinched, ever so slightly. Larry Walters made a habit of overstepping his bounds, professionally and socially, and Anna found him disgusting. He was so crude. She tried to back away, but between Mitch and the bar she didn't have anywhere to go.

"You staying long?" Larry continued. "Maybe we can get together one of these nights . . . one of these hot nights, when—"

"The lady's nights are already spoken for." Mitch's voice cut through the syrupy come-on. His grin was still in place and he hadn't moved a muscle, but Anna felt a definite change in him. As a rescue his words weren't much, but they definitely had the desired effect on Larry Walters. His hand tensed on her back, then he slowly withdrew it.

"Who's this guy?" he asked, jerking his head in Mitch's direction.

The opportunity to put Larry in his place was too good to pass up. She pretended to look surprised as she turned to him. "This *guy*?" Her voice rose and one silky brow arched. "You mean Mr. Mitchell Summers? Didn't St. John inform you of his arrival?" The first signs of doubt crossed Larry's face, and Anna knew exactly what he was thinking—his job wasn't so secure that he could afford to offend one of St. John's special guests. "Mr. Summers owns Summers Oil. *The* Summers Oil out of—"

"Denver," Mitch interrupted, extending his hand and grinning broadly.

This man catches on fast, Anna thought, throwing Mitch a shrewd glance. Larry shook Mitch's hand, and Anna had to struggle to keep from laughing out loud at the miraculous transformation in his attitude.

"We run the best tables in Nassau, Mr. Summers. If you need anything, just ask for Larry Walters." He kept pumping Mitch's hand, relief evident in every word. "None of my dealers will give you any trouble, mind you, but if you're looking for something you don't see, well, just find me. I can set you up," he added with a wink.

Anna barely suppressed an irritated sigh. Pimping on company time wasn't written into any of the employee contracts that she knew of. "I'm sure Mr. Summers will be adequately entertained, Mr. Walters," she said coolly.

"Yeah," Mitch said as he draped his arm around Anna's shoulders and pulled her close. "Old St. John is taking real good care of me."

She shot him a glare. He not only caught on fast; he moved fast.

Larry's eyes widened as he took in the proprietary action. "My, my, my . . . You and St. John must be very good friends. Yes, indeed. You just remember Larry Walters, Mr. Summers. Anything you need, just call me." He backed off, a sleazy smile curling his full lips.

The instant Larry's attention was elsewhere, Anna extricated herself from under Mitch's arm.

It didn't take any effort. He released her easily and stepped back a bit to give her more room.

"A friend of yours?" he asked, nodding at the retreating form of Larry Walters.

"Mr. Walters works here. Sometimes he forgets that," Anna said, dismissing the pit boss, and took a sip of champagne. "Thank you for helping me remind him."

"My pleasure." A boyish grin replaced the put-on one he had given Larry.

Despite her efforts to the contrary, Anna found herself responding in kind. What was it about him? she wondered. "Yes, I'm sure it was, but now I really must be going. Good—"

"Don't say good-bye."

"—night, Mr. Summers."

"Just as bad." He shrugged. "You sure I can't buy you dinner?"

She met his eyes directly, forcing herself not to be taken in by their openness or the inappropriate attraction she felt toward him. Larry Walters was a minor irritation compared to the trouble this man might bring. She didn't know yet what that trouble might be, and she wouldn't until St. John checked him out.

Slipping off her chair, she graced him with a cool smile, one designed to put them back on stranger's ground. "Good night, Mr. Summers, and good luck. Try not to take advantage of Larry Walters's apparent generosity. He doesn't own the club." She set her champagne glass on the bar and cocked her head. "One more word of advice. I've seen you play, and I suggest you stick with the slot machines. Unfortunately, they don't have a keno lounge in this casino." She knew he'd been around enough to catch the obvious insult in her recommendation, as keno was a game similar to bingo. She also knew that if he liked the front of her dress, the back was going to make his tongue hang out.

Turning on her heels, she strode gracefully away from the bar. Then some sly thought from deep in her mind made her stop and throw him a smile over her shoulder. Yes. Blatant, unadulterated appreciation was written all over his face. He shook his head in wonderment. A crooked grin lifted one side of his mouth and made her want to reassure him that the laws of gravity still ruled the earth. She shrugged off the feeling and laughed, and tossed her mane of jet-black hair as she made her way to the baccarat table.

Poker was Anna's game when she played for herself. She had two reasons for tonight's game: St. John had asked her, and she enjoyed the change of pace in playing with someone else's money. St. John would stake her, and she would keep a percentage of the take.

Thinking of St. John, she glanced around the chandelier-lit room, looking past the glitz and glamour for the man who made it all happen in Runner's Cay Casino. It only took her a moment to spot the tall, dark-haired man also headed toward the gilded cage of the baccarat table. When St. John walked into a room there was no doubt about who was in charge. He carried the banner of control and responsibility like an invisible crown. Elegance marked his every move, arrogance subdued to calm confidence. In an impeccably tailored white dinner jacket, he was the focal point of every female eye in the private room.

They noticed each other at the same moment, and St. John held out his hand toward Anna, an inquisitive light shining in his cool gray eyes. He pulled her close and bent his head to whisper in her ear.

"We need to talk before you take your place. Let's go into my office."

Anna wasn't surprised by his request. He often had special instructions before he let her loose with several thousand dollars of his money.

The solid oak door closed behind them with a resounding thud, followed by the discreet click of a special light switch. That light warned his employees not to disturb them.

"Anna, Anna, Anna," St. John said with a sigh. He dropped into his leather wing chair and gave her an expasperated look. "What is holding that dress up?"

"Willpower, big brother, sheer willpower." She smiled as she helped herself to a cognac from his private bar. The clink of crystal filled the silence, the excitement and noise of the casino a muffled backdrop behind the closed door.

"Do us both a favor and don't wear it home for Thanksgiving. Dad would tan my hide if he knew I let you run around like that." He stretched out a hand to accept the drink she offered.

Anna sat in the chair opposite his desk, a shuttered look descending over her eyes. "Is that the new mandate, then? Home for Thanksgiving?" She took a sip of cognac, then lounged back in the soft leather, crossing her legs and flicking the strap of her sandal off her heel.

St. John eyed her warily, measuring his words before he spoke. "You've been running pretty fast these last few years, Anna. I think it's time to forgive and forget."

"Oh, I've forgiven him. In his own way he did

me a favor. I just wish his timing had been better. He didn't need to make a fool out of me in the bargain."

"We've been over this a thousand times." St. John shook his head. "You were a wild child and Dad was desperate. He would have done anything to keep you from marrying that penniless duke or count or whatever he called himself. The man was an international playboy who needed a heavy transfusion of cash—Lange cash, if that was all he could get."

"You make it sound as if I were an afterthought." Her mouth tightened in unconscious self-defense. "He was in love with me, you know."

"Wasn't everybody?" St. John shrugged, then softened his words with a smile. "You were a beautiful girl, who has grown into an even more beautiful woman, Anna. And thanks to our father you're in control of your own life and your own money. Count what's-his-name would have had you barefoot, pregnant, and broke inside of a year."

"But to buy him off on the steps of the church? Good Lord, St. John, every gossip rag in the country ran picures of Dad writing out the check and shoving Antonio into a taxi."

"It's old news, honey. Nobody cares anymore."

"I still care." She did care, quite perversely. Every protective mechanism she'd developed over the years could be traced back to her wedding day. Antonio's deception had sliced her heart open then. The sophisticated woman with the cool gray eyes who sat across from St. John now would never be deceived by such childish dreams.

She swirled her drink in the glass, watching the light glint off the facets of crystal. "You don't have to play the heavy, St. John. You know I'll be there. I'm always there for the holidays." She didn't need to add the reason she dutifully showed up at her father's house every holiday. They both knew she didn't have anywhere else to go. Beautiful, rich women attracted a lot of male admirers and few female friends.

Anna often wondered if her father regretted destroying her wedding. As much of a fiasco as her marriage would have been, at least it would have kept her off the casino circuit. As St.John said, she had been a wild child. What had started as a game of spite had somehow evolved into a way of life. The time when she should have settled down had long since passed her by. If she hadn't been able to make a living at gambling it might have been different, but Anna was good at what she did.

Too good for her own sake, she thought, running her fingers along the split satin folds falling from her crossed knee.

"That settles Thanksgiving, then," St. John said. "Let's get down to business." He pulled out a sheaf of papers, and they spent the next fifteen minutes going over the gaming habits and balance sheets of all the high-stakes gamblers in the club that evening. Anna recognized a few of the names, so they spent their time on the ones she didn't know. As the last point of business, St. John opened his safe and counted out ten thousand dollars.

Anna recounted the money for him and tucked it in her purse, knowing he would escort her to the table. "One more thing, St. John. I need a favor."

He finished locking the safe before turning around. "Name it."

"A man has been following me—"

"Nothing unusual about that," he interrupted her, smiling wryly.

She shrugged a bare shoulder, as if she didn't think it was unusual either. "I think he's a reporter. He followed me from San Francisco two days ago, and finally introduced himself tonight."

St. John's eyes hardened and his voice dropped twenty degrees as he asked, "Has he been bothering you, Anna? I can have him taken care of quite easily and very discreetly."

"No, no. It's not like that at all," she hastened to inform him. Somehow the image of Mitch Summers's face really being broken upset her. "I think he's harmless. I just want you to get some information on him so I know how to deal with him. I'm not even sure he's a reporter, but I can't figure out why else someone would be following me."

St. John relaxed slightly. "If you've been wearing that dress, I can come up with half a dozen other reasons. Where were you playing in San Francisco?"

"Chinatown, Mr. Wong's."

St. John wrote down the information. "He had to know someone to get in there, and if he knows someone, someone knows him. I'll have him checked out. What's his name?"

"Mitch Summers."

"Point him out to me when we cross the room," he said, rising from his chair and offering her his arm. "Are we still on for a late supper?"

"I wouldn't miss it," she said, planting a kiss on his cheek. With a flick or her wrist she pulled his handkerchief out of his pocket and wiped off the smudge of lipstick. "You won't have much luck with the ladies if it appears you're spoken for," she said teasingly.

"I've already got a date for tonight—don't forget. I'll be by the table around midnight, and we'll celebrate with your winnings."

She laughed as he opened the door and switched off the light. "I'll be lucky to get out of here with the shirt on my back."

He shot her a dry look and an even drier smile, muttering, "I wish you *had* a shirt on your back."

As they crossed the room, Anna wondered about the life she'd chosen for herself. She was getting jaded, and that hurt a little. There had to be more to life than keeping a low profile in the fast lane, but St. John was right. She'd been running too hard to find anything else. Maybe this time she'd stay in Nassau, invest her money in Runner's Cay, and take the management position her brother had been offering her for the last couple of years. Then again, maybe not. Somehow she couldn't quite picture herself growing old gracefully as the grande dame of casino gambling.

St. John slipped his hand under her elbow as they ascended the steps to the baccarat table. Their circuitous route through the casino had failed to reveal Mitch Summers, and Anna felt a pang of disappointment as she settled into the number-four chair. If nothing else, his fresh-faced interest had been amusing.

Don't kid yourself, lady, she thought. Amusement was hardly the right word to describe her response to a simple kiss on the palm. Simple? Try again, Anna. She pulled her money out while the last hand finished playing, only half listening to St. John's whispered instructions.

The caller gave her a discreet nod of acknowledgment, and as she responded in kind she slid her glance to the other players and met a pair of soft brown eyes. A slow smile tilted her lips as disappointment melted into a mixture of pleasure and regret. He hadn't taken her advice, and she knew the game would change considerably now that she was here. A quick look around the table showed bets just above the minimum, and she would be pushing the house limit within the hour. She hoped Mitch Summers had enough sense either not to get caught up in the action or to get out.

She lightly touched St. John's arm, obliging him to lean his dark head down to her level. "Number ten," she murmured, her eyes never leaving the lean masculine face with the crooked grin.

St. John glanced to the left of the caller and leveled a glacial stare at the younger man. "If he wins enough I'll give him the name of my tailor. That tuxedo is either rented or borrowed. I hope he's already bought his ticket home." He dropped a quick kiss on the top of her head and strode away.

Anna harbored the same hopes as St. John, but wished he hadn't voiced his appraisal so callously. Though Mitch Summers might be out of his league, she didn't want to be the one to put him in his place, wherever that might be.

The suit didn't fit. It was too full through the shoulders and a shade worn on the lapels. She was surprised she hadn't noticed before. But then, except for tonight she hadn't been close enough to notice, and earlier this evening all she'd really seen were the soft eyes that were still holding her own across the table.

Mitch lifted his hand in a short wave, and for the first time Anna noticed the sultry blonde hanging on his arm. He turned his attention and his smile toward the well-endowed beauty, and Anna noted with distaste that there could be no doubt as to what was holding up her dress. And the woman was hanging all over Mitch like a cat who had found the cream.

You'd better enjoy it while he's still got it, honey, Anna thought, because he isn't going to last long in this game. She wasn't quite able to convince herself that it was his money the woman was interested in getting. If the movement of her hands was any indication, the blonde had something a lot more physical in mind.

Anna tried to distract herself by placing her bet and sizing up the other players, but her glance kept straying to Mitch Summers. Fortunately, the banker's hand lost, and she was able to concentrate on the deal as the shoe was passed to her until it lost again. She kept her bets below the maximum, yet made them larger than what had been placed before. She wanted to bring the game along naturally and take her time picking out the high rollers. Mitch Summers obviously wasn't one of them, but that didn't seem to dissuade the blonde.

And surprisingly enough that seemed to be exactly what Mitch was trying to do. More than once Anna saw him disentangle the woman's hands from his shoulders and other places. For a man with enough savvy to follow a woman halfway around the world he was naïvely inept at releasing himself from a pair of feline clutches. At one point Anna actually opened her mouth to say something to the woman, but caught herself just in time. If Mitch Summers was dumb enough to get taken for a ride by every blond siren who came along, that was his problem. All Anna needed to know was why he had been following her, and with a name and a description St. John would have the information she needed at midnight.

If there was one thing Anna had learned in life it was not to believe what people told you about themselves, especially in casinos. It was always to your advantage to investigate an adversary from a distance and then, armed with private knowledge, meet him head on. She would confront Mitch Summers at a time and place of her choosing.

A flash of irritation at her ridiculous twinge of protective instincts toward him made her reckless with her next bet. She pushed the house limit with two thousand on the player. A murmur of excitement ran through the crowd as the cards were dealt and the caller passed the hand to her. Anna turned over the first card, a deuce of diamonds, and the second, a seven of spades. A natural nine—unbeatable.

The dealer paid her winnings, and she started to smile triumphantly at Mitch Summers, but the number-ten seat was empty and the blonde was nowhere in sight. She barely had time to register the strange feeling tightening her chest before a deep masculine voice drawled in her ear, "I did some checking with our buddy Larry and he's assured me he can get us a table for dinner all the way till dawn. But if you're tied up until then, I'll settle for breakfast."

Anna's breath caught in her throat. Her eyes slanted up to meet his, and suddenly the tightness dissipated into an uncalled-for smile. "You're terribly persistent, Mr. Summers, but I never breakfast with strange men."

"Trust me, I'm not at all strange."

She shot him a skeptical glance.

"Different, maybe," he conceded with another of those crooked grins, "but not strange."

Anna had her doubts on that score, and she knew they all showed on her face. Even if, by some outside chance, he wasn't strange, the effect he had on her was strange enough to make up for it. Maybe she'd been alone too long, she thought. The first good-looking man who walked up to her without avarice written all over his face and she was fascinated. But he did want something, or he wouldn't have followed her from San Francisco. She shook her head and placed her next bet, five hundred on the banker.

"Mind if I watch?" he asked. "I haven't really figured the angle on this game yet." He casually draped his arm across the back of her chair, moving the extra step necessary to bring his body close to hers.

She ignored the brush of his jacket against her back—almost—and the fraction of an inch separating his slacks from her upper arm—almost. "There are no angles in baccarat." The word flowed off her tongue, dropping the *t*, rolling the *r*.

"See? I've already learned something. I've been calling it *back-a-rat*, and that's about how all my hands went."

A quirky grin teased her mouth at his unpretentious summing up of his skills. The smile was completely out of character, and the man two chairs over immediately changed his bet to the banker. Anna barely subdued a chuckle and glanced up at Mitch.

"You certainly add a new dimension to the game, Mr. Summers."

"In most games, Ms. Lange." His thumb brushed across her shoulder blade, leaving a trail of warmth, and his eyes darkened. "I like to play by my own rules."

She caught the hint of challenge in his touch and his words, and her smile softened. "And if there are no rules?"

"Then I make them up as I go. It keeps things interesting."

"Yes . . ." The word came out a little too breathless for Anna's taste, but his thumb was making another circle on her skin and there seemed no armor against his touch. "It certainly does."

Their eyes met, clear gray and rich brown, taking full measure of each other.

"Mitch." A deep-throated whine broke the moment. "I'm hungry."

Mitch and Anna both looked at the blonde sidling up to him. Then Mitch's eyes came back to Anna and both his brows lifted in question. With an almost imperceptible shake of her head she answered him.

He looked at the pile of money being pushed in her direction by the dealer. "You're good," he said, more to himself than to her, as if he were confirming her prowess rather than admiring it.

His tone caught her off guard, but only an instant passed before she replied, "I know." As he walked away with the blonde she added with a heavy sigh, "Too good for my own sake."

Anna lost the next three hands as the excitement drained out of her. It was eleven-thirty, and she had half an hour before St. John would return, but the game had gone flat.

At midnight, after a series of major losses and minor wins, she cashed out, and rose from the table just as St. John appeared at her side. His glance took in the amount of money she put in her purse, but he didn't say anything until they were back in the office and returning her stake to the safe.

"Bad night?" he asked, twirling the lock and throwing a puzzled look over his shoulder.

"Let's not talk about it." She checked her face in the rococo mirror behind the bar, fluffing the spiky shag of bangs that framed her wide-set eyes and high cheekbones. A fresh spray of Magie Noire misted her collarbone as she caught St. John's eyes in the mirror and held his gaze.

"What did you find out about Mitch Summers?" she asked. Her voice held a strain of impatience that she wished weren't there.

St. John took his time answering, and the longer he waited the more she knew she wouldn't like his answer. And she didn't.

"Nothing," he said. He pulled a gold case out of his jacket pocket and lit a hand-rolled cigarillo. "Well, almost nothing, unless he lied to you about his name. Let's go to dinner and I'll tell you what I found out about a man named Stephen Summers."

Two

Anna and St. John climbed a private staircase to the second-floor dining room, where the maitre d' ushered them to a table on the balcony, overlooking a moon-washed ocean. White linen, sterling silver, and cut glass adorned the tabletop, but Anna barely noticed. Her mind was too busy racing around the fact that the man with the soft brown eyes and crooked grin had lied to her. Back to rule number one: Don't believe anything anyone tells you about himself, even if he looks as guileless as a boy scout.

It was ridiculous to feel betrayed by his lie and alternative choice of a companion, but she did. More by her own instincts than by the man. She'd felt he was different from the men she generally met. Certainly he lacked the usual pretentiousness, the guarded look in the eyes, the practiced facade.

The wine steward poured their wine, and St. John lifted his glass in salute. "Here's looking at you, kid," he said with a wry smile.

She clicked her glass on the edge of his, then settled back into the upholstered luxury of her chair. "Well, what did you find out about Stephen Summers?" The name felt awkward on her lips. He'd told her Mitch and she had believed him.

St. John swirled the Chardonnay in the long-stemmed glass, then took a small sip. He closed his eyes in concentration to taste the wine before answering her. "He's a lousy gambler—"

"I already knew that."

"—and a poor loser."

Now, that bit of information took her by surprise. The man she'd met didn't seem to take gambling very seriously, and she'd been at the same table with him twice. "Go on," she said.

"He's a lawyer in San Francisco, married, three children."

And he cheats on his wife, she thought with weary resignation, ignoring the pang of regret that came with St. John's words.

St. John continued. "He showed up in Monte Carlo a few months ago and lost a lot of cash and a substantial amount of property. The game was poker, the stakes were high, and the host was Jacques Dumonde."

Anna gasped, and almost choked on her wine as she leaned forward in her chair, a tumble of silky black hair falling over her bare shoulder. "What in the world was a San Francisco lawyer doing in a game with Dumonde?"

"Losing his shirt, by all accounts," St. John answered, shrugging.

Jacques Dumonde was a persona non grata at Runner's Cay and any other casino that wanted to make a profit. The man was a well-known card mechanic who had turned to fleecing tourists because his face had become too familiar in the clubs. Anna had played against him once in Paris, and although she couldn't prove it, she knew he'd been second dealing. He was subtle, very quick with his hands, and he had cleaned her out.

"Why do you think Summers is following me?" she asked as the waiter appeared with the first course, smoked salmon with capers and dill sauce.

St. John's gaze wandered over the other diners on the balcony as he took a deep breath and expelled it in a long sigh. "Did you cover all your bases in San Francisco?"

"Of course I did," she snapped, not bothering to hide her irritation. She knew what he was insinuating. Chinatown games weren't legal, but she wasn't a novice. "Anyway, you said he was a lawyer, not a federal agent, and we're in Nassau."

"I know, sweetheart. It was a long shot, but if it's not a legal problem, then that just leaves the dress. Maybe he's making a play for you. Salmon?" He held out a portion of the delicacy on his fork.

She took the mouthful but shook her head at another bite. "He could have made a play for me in San Francisco and saved himself a plane ticket," she said, dismissing his opinion despite Mr. Summers's obvious attraction to her.

"Then your guess is as good as mine. I'd ask him the next time I saw him, if I were you."

She had already decided to approach Mr. Summers and get to the bottom of his charade.

"There's always the possibility he isn't following you," St. John continued. "Could be he's out for a little old-fashioned revenge. Jacques Dumonde is in Nassau."

If that was the case Anna didn't want anything to do with Mr. Summers. Being between Jacques Dumonde and a poor loser was the wrong place to be under any circumstances.

During dinner their conversation turned to St. John's first love, Runner's Cay, and the inherent problems of employing a hundred people and trying to make your dream their guiding light while taking care they didn't steal you blind in the process.

Partway through dessert, the waiter approached the table, standing to one side until he caught St. John's eye. "Excuse me, Mr. Lange. Mr. Walters requests your presence on the floor."

St. John was obviously annoyed, but rose from the table. He couldn't afford to ignore his pit boss. If Larry Walters had called, it must be important. Otherwise he wouldn't have dared to interrupt St. John's dinner.

"Do you have your key to the house?" St. John asked Anna.

She nodded, and swallowed a bite before she added, "I'm going to call it a night when I'm finished with dessert. Thanks for dinner and the information."

He gave her a brotherly kiss on the cheek. "Anytime, sweetheart," he said, and turned to follow the waiter, leaving her alone to sort through her thoughts on why a married San Francisco lawyer was hot on her trail.

Late-summer breezes caressed her skin as she sipped her wine and watched the ever-changing ocean splashing on the beach. Half of the dessert went untouched. It was delicious, but too much. She closed her eyes and inhaled the tangy smell of salt spray and the sweet bouquet of seductive island flowers.

After a few moments of quiet contemplation, she sensed she was not alone. She opened one heavily shaded lid, and her gaze encountered a tuxedoed midriff. Both eyes opened and she stretched deeply into the chair as she let her gaze slowly wander up the length of worn lapels to a crooked grin and a golden face.

Her stretching caused the satin folds of her dress to slip dangerously low, inspiring a deep sigh from the white-shirted chest and a flame of anticipation in the brown eyes.

"Good evening, Mr. Summers." She rolled the words off her tongue, fully aware of the effect she was having on him. She knew the dress would only go as far as she wanted it to—but he didn't. "Congratulations on your luck at the baccarat table."

"I barely broke even." His husky voice caught as he forced his eyes up to meet hers.

"I wasn't alluding to the game." She smiled and brought her wineglass to her lips. "Please. Be seated."

As he sat down a service person appeared and whisked away all traces of her dinner with St. John. Then the waiter approached, directing his attention to Anna.

"Another bottle of the Chardonnay, please," she said. "You will join me, won't you, Mr. Summers?" She enjoyed turning the tables on him. He might have made the first move, but she was in control of the situation.

"Joining you is exactly what I had in mind, Ms. Lange." He delivered the words in his western drawl, the light still shining in his eyes.

He seemed to have regained his composure, and she was momentarily disconcerted by his confidence, but she knew it didn't show on her face or in her gesture as she graciously waved the wine steward toward Mr. Summers. Let him decide if the wine was suitable for his undoubtedly plebeian tastes, she thought.

She hid her satisfaction as he swallowed the initial small portion of wine in one gulp and pronounced it fine. With unfazed aplomb, the steward acknowledged Mr. Summers's verdict and poured full glasses for both of them before melting into the dining room, leaving them alone on the balcony in the warm Bahamian night.

Strains of music and laughter drifted up from the ground-floor casino, softly punctuated by the waves breaking continuously on the shore and the junkanoo beat of a steel band playing farther down the beach. Anna took her time before initiating conversation, knowing the first move was hers, knowing he would give it to her.

She watched the candlelight dance shadows across his face, sharpening the lean angles, highlighting the curve of his dark eyebrows, and softening the bend in his nose. In her mind she was trying to reconcile the innocent mischief of his face with the facts—lousy gambler, poor loser, unfaithful—and couldn't get the disparate images to match up. Logic told her to put her instincts on probation and go with the facts until she got to the bottom of this scenario.

"So tell me, Mr. Summers." She arched forward, delicately holding her wineglass in both hands as she leaned her elbows on the table. "Why have you been following me?"

He met her gaze straight on, the softness in his eyes reaching across the night to melt her coolness, his slow grin lifting a corner of his mouth.

"Do you believe in love at first sight?" he asked.

Her mouth curved into a cynical smile as she shook her head. "Try again," she prompted.

"Okay." His voice lifted both syllables in a long sigh. "How about this one? I need you . . . your services, Ms. Lange, for just a few hours, but I'm willing to pay for a whole night if that's what it takes."

There was nothing like good breeding to keep your mouth from falling open. His outrageous proposition astounded her, but no telltale flush of anger marred the cool serenity of her face, and no whitening of her cheeks displayed her shock. Her delicate grasp on the wineglass turned into an icy grip and for a few seconds she was incapable of bodily movement, but other than that she was okay. Insulted, but okay.

Maybe the dress was too much—or too little, depending on how you looked at it, she thought. If she'd given him the impression she was a hooker, then she needed to reevaluate her wardrobe.

No, she decided, she was being ridiculous. Any mistakes had been made by him in his naïveté. She had impeccable taste. Of course, it was almost flattering to think a man would follow her halfway around the world just to take her to bed. Almost, but not quite, especially when he seemed unsure of how long it would take for her to satisfy him. All night indeed!

She set the wineglass on the table and refocused her attention on the man patiently waiting for her reply.

"You have made an error in judgment, Mr. Summers, obviously not your first." She spoke in her most condescending manner, looking up at him from under long, sooty lashes. "I don't sell the kind of services you need."

The smile slipped off his face, and his eyebrows pulled together across his smooth forehead. He was so transparent, she had to force herself to keep from laughing. No wonder he'd lost his shirt to Jacques Dumonde. Even a straight dealer could have cleaned him out.

"I know it's an unusual request," he said, his voice taking on a surprising urgency as he leaned forward. "But if you'll just hear me out, maybe you'll change your mind. This is important to me."

Where in the world was he coming from? she wondered. It sounded as if he needed a sex therapist, not the high-priced call girl he'd taken her for. She instinctively sat farther back in her chair, putting extra distance between herself and the insistent Mr. Summers.

"I'm not the woman you want. . . . Um, let me rephrase that. I'm not the woman you're going to get." She lowered her eyes meaningfully. "You should have held on to the blond lady at the baccarat table. She at least seemed willing." Anna put it as delicately as she could, hoping he would take the hint and leave. If he didn't, she was going to signal for the maitre d' to get rid of him, and if he showed up again, she would reconsider St. John's offer.

Her words were met by a quizzical look that slowly changed to understanding. The face that had been so transparent only moments before iced over in a frigid wariness, the soft brown eyes shutting her out on all but the basest level of awareness.

"You have made the error in judgment, Ms. Lange . . . obviously your first." His husky voice was as cold as his face. "I wouldn't pay two bits to take you to bed. The services I'm willing to buy are your gambling skills, specifically your poker game."

Anna felt the flush of embarrassment spread

across her chest and run up her neck to her cheekbones. Her bare skin trembled with the heat of it. She was stunned, and she knew it was written all over her face. How had she made such a stupid mistake? Mitch, or Stephen, or whatever-his-name-was-Summers had crossed her wires but good this time. The guileless face wasn't as easy to read as she'd been giving herself credit for tonight. So far he hadn't done anything but surprise her.

Good breeding told her to excuse herself politely from the table and forget she'd ever had this conversation, to wipe it out of her memory. "My apologies for misunderstanding." She forced a tight smile to her lips and stood up.

A pained grimace twisted the smooth planes of his face as a whispered curse forced its way through his clenched teeth. Before she was halfway out of her seat he reached over and grasped her hand.

"I'm sorry. . . . Please stay," he said. "I apologize for giving you the wrong impression. I should have stated my case more clearly, but lady, you do have a tendency to take a man's breath away."

With her curiosity barely edging out her good sense, Anna allowed herself to slip back into her chair. The muscles along his jaw relaxed slightly and a teasing smile flirted with his lips. He still held her hand across the white linen.

"You are beautiful, Anna Lange . . . very beautiful." His gaze dropped to their hands, his rough and blunt and dark against the slender tawniness of her own. He let his thumb glide across her knuckles as he released her. "If we can get beyond mutually offending each other, there's still a chance I can salvage my investment."

He avoided her eyes, and she could tell his crooked grin was directed more at himself than at her. She pulled her hand back and lifted her glass to her lips, trying to remind herself of his marital status. Why that should be so difficult she didn't want to dwell upon. She only knew she was becoming increasingly charmed by his self-effacing manner and the semblance of honesty reflected in those soft brown eyes, despite the facts.

She forced her attention back to the issue at hand. Her innate composure was reasserting itself, although she still felt the heat in her cheeks. "I can't help you, Mr. Summers. I just play for myself. Besides, only a sucker would try to beat Jacques Dumonde at his own game."

"Call me Mitch, please." She could tell he was being careful with her, wanting to win her over and not quite sure how to do it. "How did you know it was Dumonde I wanted you to play?"

This time it was Anna's gaze that shifted away as she fiddled with the glass stem. "I had you checked out while we were at the baccarat table. I'm aware that you lost heavily to Dumonde and also that your name isn't Mitch." A trace of disappointment was threaded into her voice. "You're not only a lousy gambler, Stephen Summers, you're a lousy liar, too. The best advice I can give you is to go home and stay away from the fast action."

"Well, you certainly have it all figured out," he drawled, relaxing his manner and his body as he slipped farther back into his chair.

"It's hot tonight, isn't it?" He tugged at a corner of his tie and let the black silk dangle down the white pleated shirt. He loosened the top few buttons, then stretched his legs out in front of him and dropped his head on the back of the chair.

"You're right, of course. I am a lousy liar. . . ." His voice was directed at the stars studding the black velvet night. "That's why I never bother. My name is Mitch, Anna. Stephen is my brother, and what he lost to Dumonde belongs to me." He lifted his head up a few inches to meet her eyes, a lock of sandy hair falling forward, contrasting with the sable of his brows. "And I want it back."

Anna carefully gauged her reaction to his explanation, letting her attention wander to the party breaking up on the beach. The last liquid notes of a steel drum floated through the lush darkness, echoing against the sea, melting into the night with the barefoot people. She wanted to believe him, wanted to believe there was some blow she could strike for justice. A mixture of relief and sadness swirled through her heart. To be swindled by your own brother must hurt, but he was no match for Dumonde, and neither was she.

"I'm sorry, Mitch. I can't help you."

"Why?" The word was barely a whisper through the half light of star shine and flickering candles.

She let out a deep sigh, lifting her heavy hair off the nape of her neck for a moment's respite from the heat.

"Jacques Dumonde is a cheat, the best. I wouldn't go up against him for my own grandmother. Try to understand. . . . You'd only lose more than you already have."

She could tell he was thinking about what she'd said, and hoped he would accept her answer. If she'd been completely honest with him, she wouldn't have made their chances sound quite so grim. True, she couldn't beat Dumonde at his own game, but she'd learned a few tricks since their last meeting.

"I had you checked out too," Mitch said. "You're good—some say one of the best. I'm willing to take a risk on you." His tone was serious, with a disconcerting edge of desperation.

Anna was feeling worse for him by the minute, but it didn't change the facts. "Why me? There are other people who would love a chance to beat Dumonde, especially with someone else's money."

"But you have an honest face."

"Is that why you followed me? Because I have an honest face?" she asked incredulously, her eyes widening in disbelief.

"I'm a great judge of character. It's one of the things I'm best at. Most of the folks I've seen hanging around these places give me the willies." He paused for a second, then flashed her an art-less smile. "You kind of give me the willies, too, but I like your willies."

"I'll just bet you do," she drawled, shaking her head, trying not to encourage him. "Okay, Mitch. Let's suppose I decide to play for you. What's in it for me? I don't need the money."

She hated the way his face brightened when she said those last words. Couldn't he see it was hopeless?

"That works out real well for me, because I don't have any money. I've worked out a plan—"

"Wait a minute," she interrupted, holding up her hand. "You want to hire someone to play a fast game of poker and you don't have any money to stake her with?" There she was, shaking her head again. "Go home, Mitch Summers," she said, dropping back in her chair.

She really hated the way his face fell. This nice guy was in deep trouble, but there wasn't any-thing she could do about it, unless . . . No, surely he wasn't going to ask her for money. She hardened her resolve and waited for his response.

"I can't go home." His eyes closed in tired resignation. "Dumonde owns it now."

Resolve went out the window as shock drained the energy from her body. She slid down in her chair in a very unladylike posture.

She moaned. "I don't believe this. Your brother conned you out of your house? I thought you said you were a good judge of character."

They both hung on their chairs like wet noodles, Mitch with dejection and Anna with a lack of sophistication she hadn't felt in years. A scent-laden breeze barely stirred the air around them. It was two o'clock in the morning and the dining room was almost empty, adding to the melancholy hovering over their table.

For the life of her Anna couldn't figure out why she was taking his problem so personally. Maybe it was because St. John was such a haven of stability in her life. If he had ever turned on her the way Mitch's brother had turned on him, she would have thrown in the towel, given up on all of humanity. And yet here was Mitch Summers, reaching out to a total stranger just because she had an honest face.

She thought about that too. No one had ever described her face as honest before. Beautiful? Many times. Honest? Never. She *was* honest, which was why her chances were slim against Dumonde. But how could Mitch Summers know it with such certainty? What had he seen in a stranger's face across a crowded casino in San Francisco that had brought him to the islands— with no money?

"It's the thing I'm third-best at, judging character," he said, slowly coming back to life, "and it's not just a house. It's a ranch that Steve and I both own, except he was supposed to sell me his acreage. Unfortunately the house sits on the land that Steve lost to Dumonde."

"Sue him," she said bluntly.

"There weren't any contracts. Code of the West, family honor, and all that." He shrugged. "Besides, I don't really blame him. Gambling is a sickness in some people, and Steve is one of those people. But I think he's learned his lesson this time. Contacting you was his idea."

"I never met your brother."

"He heard about you and saw you play at Mr. Wong's a few times."

Anna leaned forward, her brow furrowed. "You need a keeper, Mitch Summers, or a guardian angel. The man cons you out of the roof over your head and you still take his advice?"

"Not completely. That's why I didn't approach you in Frisco. I wanted to check you out first. I'm not much of a gambler, but lady, anybody could see the way you blow their socks off—in any game." He paused for a moment as he refilled their glasses. "The job of guardian angel is open, if you'd like to fill out an application."

"Where did you get the money to bankroll your traveling?"

"I took out a second mortgage on a few acres, got plenty of papers from that deal."

"At least your track record is improving. What's your plan?" She wanted to bite her tongue for asking. It was begging for trouble.

"Percentages, that's the key. I'll give you ten percent of the land you win, with a buy-back contingency. And until I buy it back you'll own some of the finest fishing rights in the world."

She couldn't believe how crazy it was. "Don't tell me," she said, shooting him a wry glance and lowering her voice until the tone was serious. "You're standing in Mr. Wong's and casually look around the room until you spot a woman dressed in diamonds and silk. Suddenly your instincts take over. You quickly judge her character and decide that there's a woman with fishing on her mind. Give me a break." She threw up her hands and laughed. This would go down as one of the most ridiculous and memorable nights she'd ever had.

Mitch Summers surprised her again by joining in with a deep laugh of his own. Moisture gathered in the corners of her eyes as she let the absurdity take her over. Mascara smudged the white linen napkin she used to wipe her cheeks. She knew she must look a mess, but she couldn't stop. Here they sat, laughing in the dark, alone in one of the most exclusive restaurants in the islands, with dawn only three hours away.

Mitch leaned forward and picked up her hand, rolling it over in his own, his mouth still wrapped around that crazy grin. "You're right again, Anna, that's exactly how it happened. I'm just glad you turned out to be the same Anna Lange I was looking for."

"I hate to disappoint you, Mitch, but I wouldn't know a rod from a reel and have even less interest in finding out." She finished wiping her eyes and dropped the napkin on the table, but she didn't pull her hand away.

She liked the feel of his work-roughened hand caressing hers. It was different from the smooth softness of the other men she met. He was different. He was masculine without being aggressive or threatening. He was so naïve she wanted to pat him on the arm, tell him everything would be okay, kiss his cheek and reassure him. She gazed at his face, lean and golden and smiling in the moonlight. Maybe kiss him on the mouth, maybe tangle her fingers in his sandy-brown hair, maybe run her hands along his shoulders to feel the strength she knew was there. He was different. He was sexy and she liked him. It wouldn't be so bad owning a piece of property outside of San Francisco. The city was one of her regular stops.

"How much is ten percent if I win?" she asked.

"Ten acres."

"In cash, boy scout."

"About twenty thousand with the cabin on it."

"And how much property are you going to give me to play with? If I decide to take you on." She added the last with a note of warning.

"A hundred acres to match the hundred Dumonde has."

"Just how much property do you own?" she asked, impressed with the numbers he'd revealed so far.

"Two hundred acres. Of course I had to mortgage a few of them for this trip."

A cold, sinking feeling invaded her heart. "You're going to risk it all?" He was more of a gambler than she'd given him credit for, and it bothered her.

"I want it all, Anna. It's my home. I worked hard for it, and I'm not about to let some two-bit hustler cheat me out of it." He wasn't laughing anymore. His voice was deadly serious, and she knew that under any other circumstances Jacques

Dumonde wouldn't stand a chance against him. But they were talking poker with a sleight-of-hand master, and Anna felt compelled to change his mind.

"That kind of property around San Francisco must be worth a fortune. Why don't you mortgage off the rest of the land and buy out Dumonde?"

Mitch released her and withdrew to his side of the table. He swept a broad hand over his face and slumped back in the chair, momentarily covering his eyes and rubbing his temples as if the whole sorry mess gave him a headache.

"I tried that. Dumonde wants more than I can raise. He's got the expensive hundred acres—river front. And the ranch isn't in California. It's near Hot Sulphur Springs, Colorado."

"Hot Sulphur Springs? How . . . uh, obscure." Where did they come up with these names? The place sounded as if it smelled bad. "Is that anywhere near Denver?"

"It's about as far away from Denver as this place is, only on the other end of the cosmopolitan spectrum. I don't think you've ever been there." He smiled again, a wry grin that told her he knew she wouldn't be caught dead in a place like Hot Sulphur Springs.

She was glad to see his mood lighten. Maybe it would help him listen to reason. "Keep the land you've got, Mitch, and make do with a hundred acres instead of two hundred. Don't risk ending up with no home at all."

Her voice held a pleading quality that made her wince. Why should she care? He was just another drifter in her world. A poor guy who couldn't afford the pace, a naïve soul who had been conned by a person he thought he could trust. It happened all the time in her world. Money could break a blood tie or a love tie. Sad but true. She didn't like it any better than he did, but he'd have to learn the hard way by losing something important. Whether it was a home or a husband didn't matter. They both hurt.

She turned her head to stare out over the dark water, mulling over the rare possibility of doing a good deed and weighing her chances against Dumonde. In truth, she couldn't have asked for a better setup; she had nothing to lose. And besides, who was she to make Mitch's decisions for him? He was a big boy.

She cocked her head to catch him out of the corner of her eye. Well, he wasn't that big. His shoulders were broad, but the body was lanky. No extra pounds there. The oversized suit made him look smaller than he probably was, and she knew he was just a shade taller than she.

"When is the game?" she asked.

He smiled. "How about getting together tomorrow night?" he drawled, letting his gaze mosey up the path of bare flesh revealed by the midnight satin.

Their eyes locked across the table. Anna's turned a smoky gray in response to the hidden question in his voice. She didn't have any control over her response, or over the warmth radiating across her skin, even though she knew he was talking about the poker game. A deep, controlled breath escaped her. She was playing with fire no matter which way she took his words.

"Give me two days," she said, "then contact me here at Runner's Cay. I'll need time to put together a scam." Her voice was cool and business-like, belying the heat he so easily and disturbingly generated with those eyes. No one would believe she was attracted to this boy scout with the broken nose. If he was her type, no wonder she'd been leading a solitary life. Boy scouts were a rare commodity in the fast track.

He looked away from her, and his mouth twisted in dismay for a moment. "I don't expect you to cheat," he said quietly.

"Listen, darlin', I'm not going in there to play a sucker's game and lose. You can be Mr. Congeniality all you want, but I have a reputation to protect." She was glad the sultry mood was broken. It put her back in charge. But she resented his innocent statement for putting her in a bad light.

"You do want your ranch back in one piece, don't you?" she asked, forcing her point home, trying to get it through his dense ignorance that her way was the only way.

"Yes, I do, Anna," he said, "and I would do anything to get it back, but I don't expect you to put yourself in a tight spot just to help me." He leaned forward and picked up her hand, holding it lightly in his own. His touch had the nicest effect on her, warm and exciting. He must like it, too, she thought. This was about the third time he'd casually reached over and played with her fingers. And for the third time she didn't pull away.

"All I'm asking for is a straight game," he said.

He was worried about her good name? She couldn't believe it. At least he didn't seem to have any scruples about the actual cheating part. The code of the West probably okayed cheating a cheat.

"Dumonde never plays a straight game," she insisted again. "What do you do if I lose?"

"I start over," he said, shrugging. "I did it once.

I can do it again. There's plenty of property for sale in the valley if you've got the price."

"But you don't have the price," she reminded him.

"No. But I've got a job and I don't want you to cheat."

"Does this job pay *beaucoup* bucks?"

"No."

She had to admire his determination and confidence, no matter how misplaced they might be. She gave him one last, long look before rising from the table. The satin folds slid over her hips as she stood. Smiling down into those rich brown eyes, she extended her hand. His handshake was dry warmth and solid strength.

"Then we'd better do it my way, boy scout . . . two days," she said, and winked before disappearing in a rustle of satin and a cloud of Magie Noire.

Three

"No, absolutely not. I forbit it, Anna. Case closed."
St. John looked up from the papers spread across
the breakfast table, but Anna couldn't see his
eyes behind the mirrored sunglasses. She didn't
need to; she knew an icy glare when she felt one.

She pulled apart another croissant and licked
the flaky pastry off her fingertips. The warm mid-
day sun felt good on her skin. Breakfast on a deck
in Nassau had to be one of earth's finest delights,
and St. John had one of the nicest decks in the
islands. It wrapped around two sides of the three-
story modern house. One side fronted the ocean
and the other was a haven of shadow underneath
the palms growing toward the shore. "I'm not
asking for permission, St. John. I'm asking for
your help."

"It's a little late for me to be explaining the facts
of life, little sister, but it sounds like you need a
refresher course. I'm St. John Lange, remember?
I own a casino. I wouldn't touch a scam with a
ten-foot pole, and you shouldn't either."

"Hah!" Anna gave a short laugh, unimpressed
by his protestations of clean living. "Let me see if

I remember this right. How about New Orleans, the Vieux Carré, Mardi Gras, about five years ago? What did you call that game? Straight? I don't think so, big brother. Or that time in Vegas? Now, that was an interesting twist on black line work if I ever saw one. And then—"

"I get your point," St. John conceded without liking it. "But I'm an owner now. I can't get involved."

"I'm not asking you to get involved. I just need your help in getting some good paper."

St. John's glass of orange juice stopped halfway to his mouth and his jaw went slack. "You cannot get away with a marked deck, Anna." He enunciated every word. "Dumonde will eat you alive."

"It's a risk I'll have to take," she said, brushing aside his concern. "It's the best chance I've got against him." A coil of hair rolled out of the pile on top of her head. She pulled out the pair of chopsticks trying to hold her hair up, and stuck them in her mouth until she could get the shiny mass back under control. Then she threaded the sticks haphazardly through her chignon, all the while patiently waiting for St. John's response.

"If that's your best shot," he finally said, "you'd better call your friend and back out of the deal."

"I won't do that." Anna spread strawberry jam on the croissant and took a bite. She knew St. John would come up with something if she kept pushing him. He had never let her down. She remembered how Mitch's brother had let him down. No. She wouldn't back out on Mitch Summers. Besides, she'd already given her word, and she never backed out on a promise. She thought about Mitch's guileless eyes and innocent face.

She doubted if he had ever broken a promise either. At least they had that in common.

St. John took his time, fingers tapping on the glass-topped table, his chin resting in his other hand. "Can you pull a 'cooler move'?"

"Not well enough to fool Dumonde, unless you could arrange a dynamite blast for a distraction, or maybe have a screaming naked woman run through the room at the exact moment I switch the deck," she said sarcastically.

He smiled. "Too obvious."

"No kidding," she said, laughing. "Come on, St. John, there has to be a way."

"Are you sure you want to do this? You don't even know this man."

"I'm not just doing this for him," she replied, hedging.

"Grudge game?" St. John asked, lifting his brow. "Or are you trying to impress Dad with the phil-anthropic possibilities of gambling? He isn't going to buy it, Anna."

She lowered her gaze and ran her finger around the rim of her coffee cup, not wanting to admit how close to the mark St. John was getting. "I just want your help."

"Okay, babe. There is one kind of paper you might get away with. A juice deck. But it will take time to get and time for you to learn how to read it. When is the game?"

"I told Mitch to contact me the day after tomor-row." She could tell by St. John's expression that he didn't think she had enough time. "We might be able to stretch it a few days. Dumonde usually likes to clean a place out before he moves on, and I saw plenty of pigeons in the casino last night."

"If you locked yourself in a room with Larry,

he might be able to teach you to read it in five days. That's cutting it short. How much is your sucker paying you for this game?"

Anna was a little embarrassed to reveal the terms of her deal, but there was no use not being straightfoward with St. John.

"Fishing rights," she mumbled into her croissant. She ignored the confused expression on his face as she got up from the table and walked over to a deck chair. She sat down, then pulled a small redwood table over for her coffee, and fluffed up a pillow.

"Run that by me one more time," St. John finally said, his voice skeptical.

"Fishing rights and ten acres of a Colorado ranch up in the mountains." She'd skip the part about Hot Sulphur Springs. The name would be meaningless to St. John anyway.

She knew he was watching her as she oiled up her body for some serious tanning, and she wasn't about to meet his assessing gaze. Let him figure it out for himself. Maybe he could explain it to her too.

He broke the silence with a low chuckle. "When did this sudden fascination with fishing come about?"

"Apparently I have 'fisherman' written all over my face. It's a latent desire I've only recently had pointed out to me," she said, intent on smoothing oil over the ninety-nine-point-nine percent of her body her black bikini didn't cover.

"He's a married man," St. John reminded her gently.

"We had the wrong man. Stephen Summers is his brother. He lost part of Mitch's ranch in the

game with Dumonde, and Mitch wants it back."
She caught the exasperated look on St. John's
face. "I know, I know. I went over every alternative
I could think of, and he still wants to do it this
way."

"Then he's a fool." St. John dismissed her new
partner with a disgusted wave of his hand.

"No," she said, gazing at him steadily over her
tanned shoulder. "Naïve, yes. Fool, no. He wants
his home back, St. John, and he's willing to take
risks to get it. You're a gambler. You can understand." She stretched out on her stomach and
reached behind to undo the string tie of her top.

St. John's silence was unnerving, but she didn't
turn around or say another word. If he wouldn't
help, they were sunk.

"Okay, Anna. I'll talk to Larry Walters."

She rolled over, holding her top to her breasts
with one hand, and flashed him a brilliant smile.
"Thanks, bro. I'll let you come fishing sometime."

St. John gathered up his papers and gave her a
warning look over the rim of his sunglasses. "Don't
do me any favors, babe."

Two days later Anna wondered if St. John had
done *her* a favor. Being holed up in St. John's
darkened study under an ultraviolet light with
Larry Walters was a real low on her fun meter.
And they had three more days to get through. She
hoped they could do it without coming to blows.
Larry didn't have to work at being disgusting—it
came naturally.

Usually she just walked away from men like
him, but she needed Larry Walters, and that was
what really galled her. One thing she had to give
him: The juice deck was good, very good. After

he'd explained how the deck worked—he wouldn't tell her how it was marked in the first place—she'd automatically gone over some of her worst past games and wondered if she'd been up against a juice deck. Her ego liked to think she had been.

"Coffee break, honey," Larry said. "You're getting a little testy." He reached up and turned off the ultraviolet lamp, throwing the room into darkness. Anna let out a disgusted sigh. She knew he did it on purpose, hoping to bump against her while he fumbled for the overhead light switch. Lord, but the boy scout was going to owe her for this.

"Back off, creep." She slapped Larry's wandering hand away. Why, oh, why, did St. John put up with him? Stupid question. She knew why. Larry Walters was slimy, but he was good at his job. He could spot a con going down at one of his tables from anywhere on the floor, and the dealers knew better than to try and pull something on him. Not that it kept them from trying every now and then anyway.

Larry used the phone while she poured herself a cup of coffee in the kitchen. The working conditions might be intolerable, she thought, but her confidence about beating Dumonde was rising with each lesson. A small smile tilted her lips. Oh, yes, Dumonde was in for a surprise. Her smile faded as Larry sidled up next to her and poured his own coffee.

He took a slow sip and leered over his cup. "Hate to disappoint you, honey, but I've got a dealer out so I'm going to have to cut our lesson short today. Same time tomorrow?"

"Let's make it ten o'clock instead of nine." She

smiled sweetly. "I don't want to take a chance on losing my breakfast too early."

He returned her smile with a toothy grimace. "You're cold, lady, real cold."

As soon as he left, Anna set down her cup and went into her bedroom to change into a pink-and-aqua-striped one piece swimsuit. A strenuous swim in the ocean was what she needed to clear her mind, and some sunshine wouldn't hurt either. Being cooped up in St. John's study on a glorious day was a sin.

The sand was deliciously hot beneath her feet, and Anna stopped to dig her toes in. She rested her arm on her forehead to shade her eyes as she stared out over the water, blue and green and full of mystery even in the light of day. St. John had promised to teach her to dive if she stayed around long enough for him to get some time off. Once again the thought of pooling her resources with St. John's came to mind. And once again it didn't feel right. Working with Larry Walters these last couple of days had pointed out everything she didn't like about the casino game. Poor little rich girl with no place to go, she thought, and laughed at herself. She didn't have it so bad.

A frothy wave broke over her feet, and she strode into the sea, pushing her legs against the water until she was up to her thighs and could dive under the waves. Strong, even strokes took her out toward the horizon. After a hundred yards she stopped and treaded water, looking back at the shoreline while the salty water lapped at her face and buoyed her weight.

Someone walked out of the glass doors of the house onto the deck, a man's silhouette against the bright white walls. From this distance she couldn't tell who it was. Too short for St. John, too thin for Larry Walters. Kicking her legs out behind her, she headed for the beach.

Halfway there she paused for a breath and saw him strolling across the sand to meet her. It was Mitch, and his timing was perfect. If he'd shown up before her swim she would have doubled her price, but she'd worked out most of her animosity in the ocean. The scout was safe.

He waited on the beach with a crooked grin on his face. The sun caught glints of gold in his sandy-brown hair. His bleached cotton shirt was only half tucked into the narrow-legged jeans riding on his hips. The sleeves were rolled up, revealing the tanned and veined length of his forearms.

She touched bottom and forced her legs against the breaking waves, tossing her long braid over her shoulder. He looked good in his own clothes, and the sight of him had a better-than-average effect on her libido, surprising her once again. She detached herself from the sinking feeling in the pit of her stomach and tried to figure out how he did that to her. If she could put her finger on it, she could work against it. A homeless waif was the last person she wanted to get involved with.

"Hello," she said, wiping the salt water off her face and definitely not meeting those soft brown eyes with the light shining in them.

"Hi." He bent his head to look up at her as he draped the towel around her shoulders. He held on to it for a minute to wrap her up, tucking one corner in next to her collarbone, his fingers brushing against her damp skin.

Anna absolutely refused to acknowledge the touch, pulling away from him and rubbing the terry cloth on her arms. "How did you find me?"

"Your boyfriend," he said, with just the slightest bit of question in his voice.

"Boyfriend?" She threw him a puzzled frown, and then, seeing a ray of hope sparkle in his eyes, added with a sly smile, "Which one?"

"The old one," he drawled, emphasizing old. "The honcho at the casino with the gray in his hair and the eyes like yours."

"Oh, that boyfriend." She nodded before drying her face on the towel. "That particular boyfriend also happens to be my brother, St. John. He owns Runner's Cay."

"Oh." A slow grin spread across Mitch's lean face as he shoved his thumbs into his front pockets and rocked back on his bare heels. "What kind of name is Sinjin? Oriental?"

"No. English. It's pronounced Sinjin, but it's spelled St. John." She tied the towel around her waist. "Come on up to the house and I'll fill you in on the game plan."

Anna undid her braid, shaking out the wet mass, as they walked up the beach. Mitch pulled a hand out of his pocket and reached over to help her, casually threading his fingers through the silky tresses at the nape of her neck, lifting and separating them as he matched his long-legged stride to hers.

She didn't take offense at his gesture. He did it the way an old friend would, helpfully. He sure was a toucher, she thought, and he sure was easy to be with—except for the twinges of excitement she felt at all those touches. But she could work around those. Being attracted to someone and doing something about it were two completely different animals.

They reached the deck, and Anna started to toss her towel on a chair, but Mitch caught it in midair and threw it over his shoulder.

"I think we can take Dumonde for everything he's got," she said, walking over to a shower head installed on the back of the house. "Including your ranch." She stepped under the shower and pulled the chain, unleashing a wall of fresh water to wash away the salt.

"How's that?" Mitch asked, taking the chain out of her hand and holding it for her.

Water splashed on his jeans, and one sandy, bare foot rested in a growing puddle. His other foot was propped against the wall, his body totally relaxed as he leaned on the white wooden planks.

Anna didn't reply. Instead she closed her eyes and turned her face up into the spray, stretching her arms above her head to scrub her hair. The next thing she knew, a warm mouth was covering hers and the sinking feeling she'd felt before turned into a full-scale meltdown. Another surprise from the scout.

The water kept coming and so did his kiss— warm, delicious, insistent, caressing her lips and turning her inside out. Her arms dropped to his shoulders in slow motion as his tongue slipped inside her mouth ever so slowly, savoring every step of the way.

Anna was drowning in water and desire, both of them running down her body in lazy, undulating waves, washing away her resistance. Then the water stopped and desire took over as his hands encircled her waist and pulled her close into the cradle of his hips. His rough jeans pressed against her flat stomach through the thin barrier of her suit. She leaned into him, allowing the magic of his mouth to continue, working her own magic with him, believing only in the sensations flaming through her body.

Somewhere in the conscious recesses of her mind she registered the incredible potency of Mitch Summers in action. He pulled back far enough to kiss the corners of her mouth, and her hands slid down to his chest, the end of the towel clenched in one fist. She caught her breath against his mouth and chin, feeling the masculine coarseness of his skin on the softness of her lips, knowing this had to stop. She tried to speak, but failed, as he took the opportunity to slip back inside her mouth for an instant, sending shock tremors through her.

She tried again, and managed to gasp the most inane thing she could think of. "You're wet."

"So are you . . . behind the ears," he said. He proved his point by licking up the trail of moisture running along her jaw to her earlobe, where his tongue lingered with a series of quick, darting strokes.

"You're too fast," she choked out, trying to control the emotions he incited.

He nuzzled her ear before lifting his head and smiling. "And you told me to stay away from the fast action, right boss?"

"Right," she said, drawing just enough strength into her lethargic limbs to push away from him. "I'll go get you a dry towel. Help yourself to a beer or something."

She left him on the deck, taking several deep breaths as she walked to her room. She closed the door behind her and slumped against the louvered panels, her heart still pounding out a syncopated beat.

If he hadn't sneaked up on her, she might have avoided the kiss. The kiss . . . She ran over it in her mind, the warmth of his mouth lingering on hers, and her knees weakened even from the instant replay. Oh, brother. Snap out of it, Anna, she told herself. It was just a kiss. Just a delightfully erotic kiss under a waterfall, just a touching of mouths that had taken her out of herself and into a realm of magic sensation. Chemistry, pure body chemistry, she decided. There were probably a few thousand men in the world who could do that to her anatomy. And today she'd met the first—Mitch Summers, the one with the broken nose and the crooked grin, the one with the soft brown eyes and the innate intuition about how to touch her . . . It was just a kiss.

Her black bikini was a web of shadow against the Haitian cotton bedspread. She'd planned to sunbathe after her swim, but those two strips of cloth would be suicide after such a kiss.

Anna pushed herself away from the door and swept back the tendrils of wet hair clinging to her cheeks. Flipping through the contents of her closet, she picked out a filmy white skirt that had pearly buttons up the front and reached to mid-calf. The matching blouse had capped sleeves and a pastel embroidery of wild island flowers to match the pockets of the skirt. She dropped the outfit in the middle of the mahogany four-poster and peeled herself out of the swimsuit.

The lace of her camisole barely peeked above the top button of the blouse, and altogether, she decided, it was a very chaste-looking outfit, innocent armor against any passion lingering in the atmosphere. She worked her damp hair into a French braid and glossed her lips. With her hand on the doorknob she took one last deep breath, then walked out of the sanctuary of her room, still telling herself it was just a kiss.

Mitch stood at the rail of the deck, staring out at the ocean. As she stepped through the glass doors, he looked over his shoulder and a lazy smile spread across his face, crinkling the corners of his eyes and dazzling her with its boyish sensuality. Now that she knew what his mouth could do to her, she couldn't take her eyes off the curve of his lips and the flash of white teeth behind them. A shaft of heat went right from her throat down her middle as she remembered the feel of his teeth beneath her tongue. Delayed reaction.

She thought about turning around, going back in the house, and trying to come out again without looking at him. Instead she pretended she was facing him across a poker table, and her instinct for survival took over, cooling down her emotions and erasing the animation on her face. She met his eyes across the deck and knew he understood what she was doing, shutting him down in the only way that seemed to work.

"The game is on Friday night," she said. "Dumonde will be there along with a few others, a couple of businessmen on vacation whom he invited—I'm sure in hopes of fleecing them—and an old friend of mine who'll be in on the con." She took a seat in the shade of the brightly striped umbrella over the table. "The tourists are on their own and Nick will take a cut of the cash I win. The land is yours, minus my ten acres."

"Sounds good," Mitch said, pushing himself away

from the rail. He flipped a chair around, swung a leg over the seat, and sat down, facing her across a pair of tanned arms. A pair of arms whose imprint she could still feel around her waist and up her back. "What did Dumonde say when you told him about the land?"

She forced her gaze away from his body, hoping she didn't look as dumbfounded as she felt. He had brought out a beer for her, too, along with a couple of frosted glasses from the freezer. She was surprised that he had known to look for them. She poured her beer and took a swallow before answering his question.

"I haven't talked to Dumonde. Nick set up the game and told Dumonde he had a player interested in the property. He'll be ready to put the deed on the table when the time comes."

Mitch's eyes glazed over in thought for a moment, and his face became serious. "I have some cash left, Anna. Do you need it to get the game going?"

"No." She shook her head. "With your property backing me, I'll have everything I need." She wasn't about to tell him that she and Nick had set up a deal of their own. They'd both go in with a few grand to bait the trap, confident of winning in the end.

"What makes you so sure we're going to win?" Mitch asked.

She let out a deep sigh. "I've done my best to get the odds in our favor, but . . . there are no guarantees. You can't con an honest man, Mitch, because he's not out to get something for nothing, but you can con a cheat like Dumonde, provided he isn't running the same scam you are. Believe me, we'll be up a creek without a paddle if he catches on to what we're doing and knows how to . . . uh, play along." She stammered over her explanation, not wanting Mitch to know exactly what they were up to. Sure, he knew she was going to cheat, but something about his face made her want to keep the details to herself.

"Should I wear my tux Friday night?" he asked.

She shot him a quick glance as she reached for her beer. "Wear whatever you want. You're not coming with me."

"Wrong, boss," he corrected her. "I'm not letting you go in there alone."

"Wrong, scout," she retorted. "And I won't be alone. Nick will be with me."

"Who's this Nick guy?" His voice was leery with doubt.

There was only one way to nip this in the bud, she thought, watching a proprietary frown form on his face. "Nick Torrey. He's my other boyfriend . . . the young one."

The lie didn't come easily, but she knew Nick would back her up if she needed him. He had been trying for years to get their relationship past the platonic stage.

Mitch mulled over her statement, staring at some distant spot on the horizon, then looked back at her. "Does this mean we can't have dinner together tonight?"

Disappointment was written all over his face, and Anna wondered if he had any capacity at all for hiding his feelings. Half of the human race—the half she dealt with—depended on artifice for emotional survival. Obviously Mitch Summers came from the other half. She was distinctly uncomfortable lying to that face, so she avoided elaborating on her story.

"I'll see you after the game on Friday—to give you back your property, I hope; maybe to break some real bad news." It was better to keep all the cards on the table, where those wide, innocent eyes could see them clearly. "Where are you stay-ing?"

"The Colonial," he said, naming one of the cheaper hotels.

"I'll see you Friday, then," she said, and stood up. Solidifying the deal seemed to call for a hand-shake, so she stuck out her hand. Mitch met her halfway, holding her hand without shaking it as he rose from his chair and swung his leg over it.

They stood there for a few moments, holding hands and looking into each other's eyes, and Anna felt the tug and pull of his magnetism. Her gaze inadvertently slipped to his mouth, and as if in response to her thoughts he smiled, an open invitation for her to follow through on what was running through her mind. She was beyond smil-ing as her pulse quickened and her heart seemed to rise to her throat. With an effort of will her body rebelled against, she dropped his hand.

"It will be late Friday night," she said. "Don't worry if I'm not there before two or three in the morning."

"I won't," he said quietly. Not taking his cue to leave, he didn't move back an inch.

Anna couldn't seem to move either. They were both waiting, and as the seconds passed a tangi-ble tension filled the air between them. The situa-tion was ridiculous, and set her sophistication back a few hundred years. Finally she made a motion to break the spell. Turning her face away she started to say good-bye, but before the word could form on her lips he lightly touched her under the chin and lifted her face as his mouth lowered to claim her lips.

It was a sweet kiss, undemanding, different from the kiss under the shower, and it was over much too soon. Without another word he turned and left, walking off the deck and down the beach. Anna watched him every step of the way.

Four

"Anna, you can never have too many bikinis. The seawater absolutely eats them alive. Come on, try this red one on," Robby insisted, holding the strings of cloth up to his shirt. "That black thing you love is in rags. Personally, I always have a least a dozen extra suits on hand. You never know when a friend might need to borrow one."

"I'm not loaning you my black bikini," Anna said as she continued flipping through the rack of swim-wear.

"I'm hardly asking, darling. Your suits wouldn't fit me anyway. We're built rather differently, if you haven't noticed." Robby paused to compare her softly rounded figure to his own slim angles, then added with a smile, "You're too hippy."

A low chuckle escaped Anna as she picked out a jewel-toned blue bikini with a matching pareu. Robby's phone call had been a delightful interruption to another morning with Larry Walters, and Anna had been only too happy to call it quits and go shopping with a good friend. Whether he was listening to her problems or giving handy advice, Robby always lifted her spirits.

"I'm going to try these on," she said, plucking the red suit out of his hands, "then let's get some lunch. There's a new café in Rawson Square, near the Straw Market. They've got great cappuccino."

"Sounds divine. Let me see both of them on, but I can tell you right now, the red one's a knockout."

Anna lifted her brow in a "we'll see" look and slipped into the dressing room. The two parts of the red suit were held together by an intricate wrap of ties around the waist and up behind her back. She put it on and took a look in the mirror. Robby was right. The suit would be hard to beat.

She stepped out of the dressing room and found Robby sorting through a rack of sport shirts. "Well? What do you think?"

He lifted his shoulders with a wave of his hands. "Can I pick them or can I pick them? Don't even bother with the blue one unless you want both. That suit was made for you, Anna. What do you think of this?" He held up a pastel knit shirt. "I think this blue is my best color."

"I saw the same thing on Bay Street for half the price."

"Did it have a reinforced placket and double pockets?"

"Um-hm." She nodded.

"Great. We'll pick it up after lunch. Go change and I'll have Sara write up the suit—my treat."

"You don't have to do that, Robby."

"Consider it a belated thank you for coming to my rescue last year. Believe me, Anna, without your help after the hurricane I wouldn't be in a position to buy you anything."

"That was a business loan, and you've paid it off with interest. Seeing you succeed is enough thanks for me. I hope you're keeping your insurance premiums up-to-date. Remember, I'm still a one-percent owner of Sand Bay."

"And I have renamed one of the cottages in your honor—Analan. It's my favorite, hidden in the palms, with a private path to the beach. It's yours whenever you want it. If you'd like to come out to Eleuthera on this visit, I don't have it booked again until mid-November."

"Thanks, Robby. I'll think about it." She gave him a quick hug before heading back into the dressing room.

Window shopping took them an extra half hour on the way to Rawson Square, which put them in the thick of the lunch crowd. Robby slipped the hostess five dollars for a good table on the patio so they could indulge in his favorite pastime, people-watching. Two cruise ships had docked that morning, and there were lots of tourists to watch.

"I love these day trips to Nassau," he said. "Look at that lady over there, the one in the sailor suit. I don't know what comes over people when they hit the islands. They lose all sense of fashion. There should be a law against anyone over the age of twelve wearing a sailor suit." He sipped his rich, creamy coffee. "She could save that dress by getting rid of the collar and the scarf."

Anna nodded in agreement. "Why didn't you go into the clothing business? Anything has to be easier than running an out-island resort."

"Me and fashion? Cliché, Anna. I like the rough-and-tumble image of innkeeping." He gave her a wink and a teasing smile. "Enough of me. What's going on in your life? New man?"

She laughed. "Not even an old man."

"For shame. You have to make love, not save

love. Life is going to pass you by if you're not careful."

"Yeah," she whispered, suddenly feeling the lightness going out of her mood. She lowered her gaze and idly stirred the whipped cream into her cappuccino.

"So . . . there is a man. Why the downcast look? Unrequited?"

"Not exactly," she said, hedging. "We haven't gotten to the requiting stage. I don't want to make a mistake, and this guy has 'wrong for me' written all over him."

"Another Antonio?" Robby asked gently.

Anna smiled at the erroneous comparison. "No. Mitch is all sweetness and light. He couldn't lie his way out of a paper bag. He's the quintessential boy scout, and, let's face it, Robby, I'm hardly anyone's idea of a girl scout. But it doesn't really matter. I'm doing him a favor, and we'll leave it at that. I barely know the man."

"Sounds to me like you know him pretty well. I could give you a few merit badges if that would help."

She picked up on the humor in his tone and ran with it. "Are they giving badges for baccarat and craps now?"

"They do in Nassau. You could go right to troop leader." He lifted his cup in a mock salute. "To the Scouts."

"To the Scouts," Anna echoed, touching her mug to his.

They each took a solemn sip before bursting into laughter.

"So much for the Scouts," Robby said. "What you need is a real man." He twisted around in his chair and perused the crowd. "No playboys, no beach bums, no cruise-ship dandies."

"And no destitute waifs," she added, determined to convince herself more than Robby.

Robby gasped theatrically, one hand fluttering to his throat as he gave her a shocked look. "My goodness, is this Mitch—heaven help him—actually poor?"

"Very."

"Well, it's absolutely unforgivable." Robby settled back in his chair and continued in a conversational tone, "No person in his right mind would be poor."

Anna's brow furrowed at his flippant remark. This was a side of Robby she'd never seen, a snobbish side, and she didn't like it. She also felt compelled to tell him so.

"We've been friends for a long time, Robby, and I'm surprised at your attitude. Just because a person doesn't have any money doesn't make him the dregs of the earth. People have a lot more to offer one another than Swiss bank accounts."

"Exactly." Robby dropped the theatrics and stared at her long and hard. "Of all the women I know, you would have been the last I'd pick as the one who chose her beaux on the basis of their checkbook balances. Frankly, I'm disappointed."

His words hurt, cutting her right to the core. Mitch's poverty wasn't the reason she didn't want to get involved with him, she thought. Or was it? No, she defended herself, she wasn't that shallow. She and Mitch Summers were incompatible on many levels, of which lifestyle was only one. Besides, she didn't know why she was worrying about it in the first place. They had a business arrangement, and whatever the outcome, when it was wrapped up, their relationship would be too.

Sure in her own mind of her reasoning, she countered Robby's accusation. "Money has nothing to do with it. But if it did, you could hardly blame me, after Antonio."

"Four years is a long time to carry a grudge. Your problem is, you're spending too much time in the rarefied atmosphere of the Côte d' Azur and Runner's Cay. You need to get out and meet men who work at regular jobs. They're a different breed, and you might find you like them." Robby's gaze strayed over her shoulder, and he smiled as he pointed in the direction of the Straw Market. "Now, there's a likely-looking prospect for home-spun values."

Anna followed the direction of his hand, her gaze settling on an obese man decked out in madras shorts and a garish flowered shirt. "Too fat," she said.

"Not that one, darling. The other one." Robby's theatrics returned with his good humor.

Other one? Anna took a second look, and her jaw went slack. Lean hips, faded jeans, half-tucked shirt, with sandy-brown hair falling over the collar. Mitch.

"He's looking this way," Robby said. "I'll wave him over."

Anna lunged for Robby's hand, but she was too late. Mitch had seen her and was already walking toward the cafe patio, a broad smile on his face.

"Oops," Robby said. "Sorry, honey. He's got a broken nose. I'll tell him I made a mistake and get rid of him. He sure looked good in profile, though." Robby paused for a moment, watching Mitch's approach. "Actually, he looks pretty good even with a broken nose."

"Stop it, Robby," Anna hissed. Her smile was forced as she stood up to greet Mitch. "Doing a little shopping, I see," she said, nodding at the woven straw hats he was carrying.

"Hi, Anna," he said, reaching for her hand and holding it a trifle longer than was necessary for a greeting.

"You two know each other?" Robby asked, noticing the lengthy handclasp. "How convenient."

Mitch turned to the other man with a quizzical glance. He released Anna's hand and held his out for a shake. "Mitch Summers. You must be Nick."

"Nick Torrey?" Robby's eyes widened as he took Mitch's hand. "Goodness, no. I'm Robby Grange."

Mitch's eyes did a quick shift from Robby's handshake to Anna's face, and a grin curved his mouth. "Nice to meet you, Robby."

"The pleasure is all mine, I'm sure." Robby smiled as he dropped Mitch's hand and gestured to an extra chair. "Please join us. We're just getting ready to order some lunch. Your first time in the islands?"

"How can you tell?" Mitch asked, settling into the chair.

"Only first-timers buy the hats. Looks like you've got enough there to outfit a whole army."

"You're close. They're for my scout troop back home."

Robby rolled his eyes in disbelief. "Don't tell me. You're a troop leader. Anna mentioned you were a boy scout, but I thought she meant something else."

Anna wanted to slide under the table. If there

was any way she could have discreetly strangled Robby, she would have done so with relish.

"Oh? What else did Anna mention about me?" Mitch asked, his face full of innocent interest.

"Only that you—" Robby stopped abruptly, then smiled tightly. "Here comes the waiter. I always recommend the fresh catch of the day. I'm sure it's divine."

Anna's heel kept up a steady pressure on Robby's foot in a warning he couldn't miss. "Try the cappuccino, Mitch," she said. "Robby and I were just saying how good it is here." She smiled sweetly.

"Very good," Robby said as he jerked his foot out from under hers.

He signaled the waiter and ordered another round of coffee before continuing the conversation in a less-hazardous vein. "How long are you staying?"

"Anna and I have some business to attend to on Friday. Depending on how it goes, I'll either leave Saturday morning or spend a few more days sightseeing."

"You should have Anna bring you out to Eleuthera. I own a resort there, and I've already offered her one of the cottages. The two of you could have a wonderful time. Swaying palms, moonlit beaches . . . We have it all at Sand Bay, and I was just telling Anna she needed a—"

Anna aimed a desperate kick at Robby's shin, but it was Mitch who winced and grabbed his leg.

"Excuse me," she said with a gasp, thoroughly embarrassed.

"I'll live."

"Darling," Robby drawled, "I don't think I've ever seen you blush."

She shot him a "drop dead" glare and turned to Mitch. "I'm sorry."

"It's okay," he assured her, still rubbing his shin.

"Goodness, look at the time," Robby said. "I'll have to skip lunch or end up on a mailboat. It's been delightful meeting you, Mitch." He held out his hand. "I'll expect both of you on Saturday. But if Anna can't make it," he added with a coy smile, "you're welcome to come on your own."

The innuendo of his words wasn't lost on Anna, and she was surprised at the fleeting spark of anger she felt.

"We have a wonderful cook at Sand Bay," Robby continued. "I'll treat you to a Bahamian feast." He stood up and kissed Anna on the cheek, then backed away from the table. "Remember what I said about life, dear. Some things are worth the risk."

In a flurry of words and waves he was gone, and Anna and Mitch were left alone at the table. She watched Robby disappear into the crowd, until politeness insisted she face Mitch and say something.

"Looks like you've made a conquest," she said. "Robby doesn't offer free rent to every pretty face he meets." She meant the remark to embarrass him, but Mitch's chuckle didn't sound embarrassed.

"Pretty face, huh? Is that a personal opinion?" He leaned back in his chair and stretched his legs out next to hers.

"You know what I mean," she said huffily, snapping her menu open. Taking a deep breath, she tried to corral her thoughts. Figuring out Mitch Summers was becoming a full-time job, and one she had yet to master. Most men would have been offended by Robby's faintly veiled proposition. That Mitch wasn't offended meant one of two things: He was either very assured about his masculinity or, knowing Mitch, he didn't realize he'd been propositioned.

She peered at him over her menu, scrutinizing the ageless face with the boyish grin and twinkling eyes. "Do you even know what was going on?"

He shrugged. "I think your friend made a pass at me."

Well, at least he got that part right, she thought. "And you're not offended?"

"Jealous?" he asked in a softly teasing tone.

"No," she snapped, knowing he was uncomfortably close to the truth. "But most men would feel threatened by Robby's invitation unless they were . . ." She gave him a startled glance as the thought went through her mind.

His grin faded. He leaned forward and cupped her face with one hand, pulling her toward him with gentle force.

Anna didn't have time to react before his mouth descended on hers. The clatter of plates and the sound of a hundred chattering voices disappeared as their lips met and his tongue trailed across her mouth, caressing and teasing with an easy pressure. She responded in spite of herself, opening her mouth to receive the full sweetness of his kiss. The melting feeling he inspired was too seductive not to explore.

His fingers tangled in her hair, urging her closer, as his other hand grasped hers on the table. Their fingers entwined, and his thumb stroked hers in tempo with the forays of his tongue into her mouth, pulling them nearer to the edge of desire.

Anna fell deeper into his web of sensual enchantment, forgetting the café, forgetting the noise, forgetting the warm sunshine as she followed his lead into the magic of the kiss.

"Ahem. May I take your order?"

The request came from another world, a world Anna didn't recognize until Mitch broke away with a reluctance echoed in her own heart.

"You are too special," he whispered, gazing longingly into her eyes.

"Two specials it is, sir," the waiter said as he snapped his ticket book closed and walked away.

Dazed by the ease of her response to Mitch's kiss, Anna let her gaze roam over his face. She ran a delicate fingertip along his bottom lip, and a heartbeat passed before his mouth curved into a grin.

"Is there any doubt in your mind who I want to make love with?" he asked in a husky drawl.

She slowly shook her head from side to side. "Women. No doubt about it."

"Not women, Anna . . . woman," he corrected her. "You, Anna."

The summer breeze carried the name from his lips to her heart, filling her with a yearning for more—more of his words, more of his touch. But a part of her heart still didn't believe, couldn't believe the feelings he inspired, didn't want to believe the feelings he revealed. "Why me, Mitch?" she asked softly.

He released her hand and settled back in his chair. He broke their visual contact by glancing out at the crowds, and his fingers tapped a steady rhythm on the tabletop. Anna wondered if he would answer her question at all.

"That's hard to explain," he finally said, and sighed heavily. "Especially to a woman who doesn't believe in love at first sight."

"You can't be in love with me. You don't even know me."

"Okay, Anna. Forget about being in love." A sly twinkle lit his eyes as he met her serious gaze and leaned forward. "How about just making love?"

His suggestion was enough to bring another blush to her face, and she was grateful that the waiter's arrival with their lunch saved her from the necessity of a reply.

She looked at the pasta salad set before her and frowned. "I don't remember ordering this," she said to the waiter.

"The gentleman ordered for you, ma'am. Two specials." He flipped open his ticket book and showed it to her, as if that settled the matter. "Would you like another cappuccino?"

"No, thank you. I think I've had enough."

"And for you, sir?"

"Beer, please. Whatever is on tap."

The waiter moved to another table, and Anna concentrated on moving pasta shells around on her plate, ignoring Mitch's steady gaze. After a few minutes of embarrassed discomfort she decided to take the conversational lead.

"Do boy scouts still rub sticks together, go camping, and all that other stuff? Colorado must be wonderful for camping."

"Mostly we use matches now, but camping is still a big part of scouting, especially with my troop," Mitch said, following her lead. "I'm not really a troop leader. I just help out with the major camping trips. I hope that doesn't lower me in your estimation."

She caught the flash of a crooked grin out of the corner of her eye. "I'll try to hide my disappointment, considering you're about as close to a troop leader as I'm ever going to get."

"We could get a lot closer if that would help."

"That's a very generous offer," she said dryly.

"We scouts are a very self-sacrificing bunch, invaluable to have around if you're ever in a jam."

"Next time I'm in one I'll give you a call."

"How about tonight?"

She stabbed a piece of artichoke heart and cocked her head, making sure he didn't miss the determination in her eyes. "I thought the motto was 'Be Prepared,' not 'Be Persistent.' "

"Sometimes persistence is the best preparation."

A profound realization slowly dawned on her as she perused his attractive face and relaxed posture. She had been mistaken when she'd written off his laid-back style as nonaggressive. Mitch Summers was as aggressive as they came. He was just a lot friendlier about it than most people. He was moving in on her from every angle, at every opportunity, and she liked it, even if she was unsure of the outcome. She couldn't remember another time in her life when a man had stolen kisses so easily, or when she'd enjoyed them so much.

It doesn't mean he's right for you, she reminded herself. Physical attraction might be an important part of a relationship, but it certainly wasn't enough. As far as she could tell, it was the only thing they had going for them. Still, it was an interesting situation, very interesting.

"So tell me about camping, Mitch. I've never been camping. St. John and I went on safari in

Kenya a few years ago, but we had a cook, guides, tents you could stand up in. I have a feeling you and the Scouts do it a little differently."

"Africa." The word rolled off his tongue with a touch of envy. "I'd love to go to Africa . . . Australia . . . Hong Kong. Lots of places I haven't been. Is there anyplace you haven't been?"

She thought for a minute. "Hot Sulphur Springs," she said with a smile. "I've never been to Hot Sulphur Springs, or Alaska, or Moscow. I guess you could say I've never been to the cold places."

"I'll make a deal with you. You take me to Africa and I'll take you to Hot Sulphur Springs. First-class accommodations, and I'll do all the cooking. Deal?" He held out his hand.

She lifted one finely sculpted brow in a look of pure skepticism.

He sweetened the offer. "I'll even throw in a bona fide wilderness camping trip, with a tent you absolutely cannot stand up in."

Laughter bubbled up from deep inside as she grabbed his hand and gave it a hearty shake. "Deal. But first you'd better tell me about camping. I always like to know what I'm getting into."

"You'll love it, Anna. You're a natural-born camper, I can tell."

"Another judgment call?"

"Yeah." A grin flashed across his face as he met her eyes. "You're going to love camping with me. First you start with a map, then you pick a mountain or two, preferably with a trout stream close by, and then you pack your gear. Packing the gear . . . that's the important part."

He warmed to his subject with an enthusiasm that enticed her as much as the pictures he wove with words. Vistas of clear mountain mornings and pine-scented forests came alive for her in the balmy, Bahamian afternoon. She knew they were teasing each other, that they would never share a cup of coffee around a crackling fire, with the darkness closing in, or together hear the slap of a beaver's tail on a high mountain pool, but it was a lovely fantasy and a wonderful way to spend an hour or two.

After he'd finally dragged them home with a creel full of cutthroats, Anna sporting a blister or two from their days on the trail, she took him to Africa, where the stars shone the brightest and the Serengeti stretched farther than the eye could see.

Halfway up the Never Summer Range in Colorado, they'd ordered a bottle of Chenin Blanc. As Mitch poured the last of it into her glass, they walked out of the heat in Africa, sunburned and tired, and boarded a slow boat to China and Hong Kong, having decided the fantasy was too good to end. Unfortunately the waiter had other ideas, such as going home.

He delivered the check with an authority that would brook no further delay. Anna and Mitch reached for it simultaneously, but Anna insisted.

"Then dinner's on me," Mitch countered.

As they stood up he gathered her in his arms and hugged her close to his chest. "Halfway around the world and not a single argument. I knew we'd be good together," he whispered in her ear, then gave her the lightest of kisses.

Sunshine, wine, and Mitch Summers had taken all the rough edges off Anna's world. She wrapped her arms around his waist and snuggled her head under his chin, soaking up the warmth and sturdiness of his body. This must be what it was like to truly be in love, she thought. Easy and natural and fun—and a little unsteady on your feet.

His hand rested on her hip as he guided her off the patio and into the square. "Come on, memsahib. Let's drop these hats off at my hotel and find a cozy place for dinner. Look." He pointed into the distance toward the harbor. "You can almost see Hong Kong on the horizon."

The Colonial Hotel stood on Bay Street. It's blue, shade-filled verandas stretched along both floors of the white frame structure. His room, Mitch told Anna as they walked along a stone path winding under lush palms, had a view of the garden courtyard rather than the more expensive view of the ocean. Then he abruptly released her hand and stepped ahead of her.

"I've always wanted to do this," he said, picking a blossom from a flowering hibiscus.

"Steal flowers?" Anna asked.

He approached her slowly, twirling the flower between his fingers, his eyes half closed and twinkling with mischief.

"Steal a flower . . ." he admitted, his hand smoothing her hair back from her face as he tucked the flower behind her ear, ". . . and steal a kiss."

His actions followed his words. He lowered his mouth to hers and let his hand brush against her cheek before he slipped it into his pocket, holding her with just a kiss.

Anna quickly found she needed something more to steady her world. Raising her hands a few inches, she held on to the first solid thing she touched, Mitch's hips, and as he deepened the kiss her fingers curled up and around the waist-band of his jeans.

He sighed in pleasure, stepping closer until their bodies touched from the curve of her breasts down the length of their thighs. Slowly he rubbed his body against hers, and with each movement she felt a shaft of heat run through her insides, melting reality into a pool of passion she wanted to drown in.

His mouth left hers, nuzzling the side of her neck—wet, warm, and enticingly erotic.

"Make love with me, Anna." The words were whispered in her ear. "Make love with me tonight."

Her body answered by pulling him closer, but her mind refused to follow. Three days from to-night he would be gone. She didn't really know him. Anna Lange didn't fall in love or into bed this fast.

The silent battle waged in her mind, dampening her desire with facts. Reluctantly she released him, allowing her hands one last caress down the sides of his hips before she let him go.

Mitch didn't move. His mouth still hovered next to her ear. The heat of his body still enveloped her.

"Why?" was the only word he spoke, gently and without resentment.

And why do you have to be so nice? Anna wondered, wishing she had something more than confusion to answer him with. Any other man would have been angry, could have called her a tease and not been off the mark. How had she allowed the situation to get so far out of hand? So far past the exchange of strangers?

"Is it Nick?" he asked, still not moving.

"No, yes . . . I don't know. I have to go home."

She backed away from him, feeling like a naïve schoolgirl for the inept way she was handling him, handling herself.

"I'll go with you."

"No . . . no." She held up her hand to stop him. "My car's only a few blocks from here. I'll be fine."

"I'd feel better if—"

"I can take care of myself," she said as she continued to back away. "I can take care of myself," she repeated, wishing she could forget about all the tomorrows and let Mitch take care of her. But she was Anna Lange, and this game of love was stacked too heavily toward failure for her to play.

Five

Diamonds or sapphires? Anna wondered. She held one of each to her ears and studied her reflection in the mirror. Her dress was a white silken sheath with a mandarin collar and long sleeves tapering to points on the backs of her hands, and every inch was covered with glittering white sequins. It fell to the floor like an icy flame, broken only by the thigh-revealing slit up one side.

Sapphires, she decided, to highlight the dramatic contrast between the dress and the shiny ebony hair piled on her head. She'd worn diamonds with the dress in San Francisco, the night she'd first noticed Mitch Summers. She frowned into the mirror, annoyed, because no matter what she'd been doing these last three days, Mitch's image had edged into her mind. Sure, he was a great kisser, but this was getting ridiculous.

She forced herself to concentrate on tonight's game. She checked the time. Six o'clock. Nick would be by in half an hour to pick her up, but he'd probably be late, as usual, and they'd have to scramble to get to his yacht on time.

Anna frowned again as she clipped the sapphire

earrings to her ears. She wished Nick had set the game up in a hotel room. It would have made the logistics easier. Boarding a boat in an evening dress wasn't impossible, just difficult. Especially when Nick, in his typically dramatic style, had moored the *Belle Fille* off the coast instead of keeping her at the marina. Controlling the room and everything in it added to their control of the game, but still, off the coast? She knew why he'd done it—for privacy—and normally she wouldn't have given it a second thought, but tonight was different. She was cheating tonight, and it made her nervous. Not good pregame nerves, but gut-tightening nerves.

She checked her makeup for the hundredth time, adding an unnecessary stroke of blush to her cheekbones. Dumonde wouldn't be distracted by her exotic beauty, but it would probably set the businessmen back on their heels. This was a game Anna knew how to play to the hilt. Conceit had no place in her assessment of her looks. Her attractiveness was a proven fact, and she knew the effect was more a function of her mental attitude than of her physical appearance. Undeniable beauty coupled with an untouchable demeanor were a potent challenge to any man. Her energies would be totally concentrated on the game, and the men's would be split between trying to take her money and wondering if they could take her too.

One more thing. She opened up the top dresser drawer and pulled out the juice deck. The cellophane wrapper and seal were intact. The deck looked new. You didn't need any special knowledge to take a deck of cards out of its wrapper, mark it, and put it back without having it look as if it had been tampered with. You just had to be careful.

A knock on the door surprised her. Nick? Early? Would wonders never cease? She placed the cards in her purse and snapped it shut, then slipped into her heels. She had to adjust one of them every few paces as she walked across the plush carpeting to the tiled foyer, because a strap refused to stay in place. She was still fiddling with it when she opened the door.

Instantly she knew it wasn't Nick. The square toes and worn leather of the cowboy boots on the other side of the threshold could only belong to one person.

"What are you doing here?" she snapped at the offending boots, the only part of him in her line of vision as she struggled with her shoe.

"It's nice to see you, too, Anna." The boots stepped into the foyer and Mitch knelt down. "Here, let me help you with that," he said, lifting her foot to his thigh.

Anna didn't have any choice but to grab for his shoulder and scowl at the sandy-brown head bent over her foot. The position exposed the full length of her silk-clad leg, and not an inch of it escaped Mitch's appreciative gaze. He took his own sweet time fixing her shoe, his warm hand gently clasped around her ankle. When he finished he let his hand run up the back of her leg to the tender skin behind her knee. He held her motionless as he slowly rose in front of her, his fingers trailing up her leg until he reached sequins.

"Nice dress," he said, a mischievous glint in his eyes.

The trail of heat he'd left on her leg had sapped

the bite from her anger, but she wasn't so dazed that she didn't have any bark left.

"Don't evade the issue, boy scout. What are you doing here?" She wished he weren't standing so close. It was difficult to deliver a scathing retort when your head was tilted up, and glaring lost its potency at such close range.

"If Dumonde is as bad as I think, you might need a bodyguard," he explained, stepping back to let his gaze travel up the length of her sparkling curves. "And, lady, you could use someone to guard that body." Soft brown eyes met cool gray ones, telegraphing a wistful message and slowly melting her insides.

Anna struggled to retain her facade of composure. What she didn't need tonight was Mitch Summers at close quarters, distracting her from the game and making her heart skip beats with those inviting looks.

"I've taken care of myself for a long time, Mitch. Your offer is appreciated, but unnecessary." She turned and walked through the living room, crossing between the slate coffee table and the rattan couch to the glass doors. Her hand rested on the silk draperies as she gazed out at the ocean. "I doubt there's anything you could do for me that I couldn't do for myself. Besides, if I thought a bodyguard was necessary, I would have hired some professional muscle."

She didn't enjoy putting him down, but it was the truth. The threat of physical violence was unheard-of in her circle, and any other possible confrontation was best handled with a cool head and a gracious manner. She didn't doubt Mitch's strength, only his ability to use it under pressure. He had a good body, but it was hardly intimidating, and combined with that sweet face it lacked even the potential of threat, broken nose or not.

She'd been watching him while these thoughts went through her mind, and was surprised at the lack of offense he was showing. Most men would have insisted otherwise, struck a macho stance, and set their jaws. But Mitch Summers wasn't like most men. He simply stood in the foyer with his hands in his pockets, shoulders relaxed, and grinned that crazy, crooked grin.

"Then I'll just come along for the ride, and I promise to let you handle yourself." He paused and did another slow sweep of her body. "It won't be as much fun as if I handled you . . . but, hey, it's your game."

The grin never left his face, and Anna found herself smiling back and shaking her head. He was something else. She wasn't sure yet just what that was, but definitely something else. She was beginning to realize fairly often, though, that he was hard to say no to.

"Okay, boy scout, you can come, but try to be unobtrusive. Try to make me forget you're there." Now, why had she said that? She could tell by the look on his face that he was reading more into it than she'd meant. Or was he seeing right through her?

"I'll try to cool my jets, boss, but I don't think that will do the trick. You like me, and when you like a person he's hard to ignore. It's natural to be aware of him, just as I'm aware of you."

"You're awfully sure of yourself."

"It's the thing I'm second-best at—knowing when someone likes me," he said with nonchalant con-viction, crossing the room to stand beside her.

Only a fool would deny the truth of what he

said, and Anna was no fool. "So you're a good judge of character and you know when someone likes you. What's your absolutely best thing?"

"I'll let you figure that one out for yourself," he said, his voice becoming husky as he tucked a loose tendril of silky hair behind her ear. The same ear he'd tantalized under the shower. "I've got a feeling you're going to find out real soon."

For every degree his voice dropped, Anna's temperature went up two. Despite her earlier assessment, Mitch Summers wasn't all sweet innocence, and a very feminine part of her was becoming more and more intrigued by the sensual promise hiding behind his soft brown eyes. Unconsciously she prepared herself for the kiss destined to come, her hand reaching up to touch the worn lapel of his tuxedo.

She'd no sooner made the gesture when they were interrupted by someone knocking "shave and a haircut" on the front door. The mood was broken, and Anna didn't know whether she was relieved or irritated. Relief was what she would have liked to feel, but irritation edged her voice as she backed away.

"That must be Nick. Excuse me."

It was, and, by some odd quirk of fate, he'd brought the sultry blonde who had been hanging all over Mitch at the baccarat table. This time, though, she was clinging to Nick, as if she were a Swedish ivy with the hots.

"Hi, babe. Looking good," Nick said, giving Anna a quick peck on the cheek. "Anna, Lara. Lara, Anna." He glanced over at Mitch. "Hi, I'm Nick Torrey."

"Mitch Summers," Mitch replied, giving Anna a confused look.

"Are you in the game tonight?" Nick asked.

"No." Mitch and Anna replied at the same time.

Nick looked at both of them and smiled. "Definitely not in the game tonight. Lara isn't playing either. Maybe you two can entertain each other while we take Dumonde to the cleaners."

Anna felt her hackles rise at Nick's suggestion, especially when she caught the grin on Mitch's face.

"No problem, Nick," he said. "We'll do our best not to disturb you." He turned to Anna and nodded toward the kitchen. "Could I see you for a minute before we go?"

Anna gave Nick and Lara a weak smile and followed Mitch into the kitchen. If events so far were any indication of how the rest of the evening was going to go, she was ready to throw in the towel and call it quits.

The café doors swung shut behind them, and Anna reached for the light switch, but Mitch caught her hand and pulled her farther into the dark room.

"You're taking this pretty well," he said. His voice was all concern as he continued backing away from the light in the foyer until they were against the breakfast bar.

Moonshine streamed through the window above the sink, bathing their faces in its silvery glow.

"Taking what well?" Anna asked, thankful she was able to articulate the meaningless question when reality was steadily slipping away and being rapidly replaced by breath-catching anticipation.

"Nick with another woman," he explained. "That one's a tiger. Believe me, I had quite a time shaking her the other night."

"Oh." She'd forgotten all about her little white lie.

Mitch watched her in the moonlight, his face passive, the crooked smile nowhere in sight. "It doesn't matter does it, Anna? Nick isn't your lover."

She'd never seen him so serious before, and she knew that whatever happened next was going to be very important.

"You don't have to protect yourself from me, Anna," he whispered. He took her hands in his and wrapped her arms around his waist, underneath his jacket. His back was strong and warm beneath her hands, the muscles moving as he gently cupped her face.

His breath was soft on her cheek. He rubbed his nose down the side of hers; then his mouth played across her delicate skin and nuzzled her lips.

"No more lies, Anna." His voice was husky, and she could feel his heart pounding against her own. "Let it happen if it feels right." The words blew around her ear, setting her on fire.

It never entered her mind to resist. She closed her eyes and opened her mouth, reaching out with her tongue to touch the line of his jaw, putting into action a thought that had been on her mind ever since his first kiss. The feel of his skin beneath her mouth electrified her pulse, shooting it into overdrive. She leaned into his body for support, and he responded by slipping one hand around her neck while he let the other one slide down the front of her dress. It left a molten trail, then seemed to brand her when it came to rest in the small of her back, holding her close.

A low moan echoed off the recesses of her mouth, and she didn't know if it was his or hers, as their lips met and opened for the fulfillment of just another kiss. Another kiss out of time, out of herself . . . into Mitch's magic.

The kiss was a sweet burning, aching with want. Mouths moved against each other in a slow dance of discovery, tasting and delighting. Mitch ran his tongue along the inside of her lower lip, then caught it between his teeth and gently tugged. And the game changed.

Anna felt his body tighten in her arms. His breath heightened to match the now-desperate note of desire running through her. She knew they should stop, and she would, soon. . . . Just one more minute, maybe two. There couldn't be any harm in letting the magic last a moment longer, in letting her fingers tangle in his hair, in letting her body move with his.

His response to her last thought in action was immediate, and Anna felt her common sense disappear on wings of delight and feminine satisfaction—then panic. She pushed away from him and caught her breath, watching him warily, her breasts rising in agitation. He shouldn't be able to do this to her so easily, make her lose control.

He wouldn't meet her eyes as he fought to slow his breathing. He held her hand, playing with her fingers, not yet willing to let her go completely. The seconds ticked by as they withdrew from each other emotionally into the silence of the beach-house kitchen. Anna became aware of voices in the living room, the pattern of moonlight on the floor, and the emptiness of the hand he wasn't holding.

Then he smiled, a crooked grin that automatically lit his eyes. "Give 'em hell, Anna," he said, dropping her hand with a reluctant shrug.

"Right, scout," she whispered, and stepped away from him, breaking the spell.

Lara was sitting on the couch, checking her face in a gold compact while Nick paced the floor. He looked up as Mitch and Anna came out of the kitchen.

He flipped his wrist and nodded at his watch. "Okay, kids. We'd better hit the road. Hope you two got everything worked out. Anna, honey, why don't you make a pit stop with your mirror and fix that sweet mouth of yours? Lara, come on, babe." He reached down and pulled her to her feet. "We'll meet you in the car. Five minutes max. Mitch, why don't you come with us, so the lady won't be tempted to dawdle . . . or worse yet, pick up where you left off? Hey! We've got a game to play!" Nick's excitement was contagious as he hustled them out the door.

It didn't take even five minutes for Anna to join them. Nick had put Mitch and Lara in the backseat of his Mercedes so he and Anna could double-check their strategy on the way to the marina. The dealer Nick had hired for the night had been okayed by Dumonde. Anna knew that having a designated dealer would put Dumonde at a slight disadvantage, but only a slight one. A good mechanic could do things with the cards if he didn't even handle the deck. She and Nick would be operating with a disadvantage too. They wouldn't have as much control over the timing of the use of the juice deck.

Anna carefully listened to everything Nick was saying and managed to hold up her end of the conversation, but in the back of her mind she was comparing the handsome, dark-haired man in the expensive white linen suit with Mitch. Of the two, Nick was certainly the more striking, with his classic profile, deep blue eyes, and confident sophistication. But Anna had never panicked in his arms.

Mitch Summers seemed to pull at a different part of her, though, a part she wasn't sure she was willing to explore. His honesty was frightening. He wanted to reach into the heart of her, expecting to find truth and goodness, and Anna didn't want him looking that close. She was afraid he'd come up empty-handed.

A quiet, derisive laugh escaped her as her fears came into focus, and Nick glanced at her in confusion. "Want to let me in on the joke?"

"This joke's on me, Nick," she said, refusing to acknowledge the moment of silence in the backseat. She knew Mitch was concentrating on her, ignoring Lara's blithe chatter. A trace of anger buoyed her determination as she mentally started preparing herself for the game. She didn't have anything to apologize for. If Mitch Summers wanted to breeze through life clouded by delusions of innocence, that was his problem. She was Anna Lange, all grown-up and good at what she did.

The night was warm, with a hint of wind, salty and humid, floating through the air as they pulled up to the docks. The tide slapped against the moored boats, setting them creaking, and rocking them on the water in individual rhythms. Anna made a point of stepping out in front with Nick when they walked down the wooden planks, holding onto his arm for support in case she caught her heel. The message was clear, and she hoped Mitch would believe it.

One of Nick's deckhands was there with the speedboat to take them out to the yacht. The dealer, Frank, was waiting for them on the dock. The roar of the speedboat's engine made conversation impossible during the fifteen-minute ride across the harbor, so Anna used the time to run the marks of the juice deck through her mind.

They pulled alongside the *Belle Fille*, and Nick helped tie the boat off as Mitch handed the ladies up on the deck. Anna felt nothing at his touch. She was back in control.

The game was set up in the main salon, a plush lounge paneled in teak, with brass appointments and windows on three sides. On the fourth side was the galley, where Nick showed Lara the setup for hors d'oeuvres and bar supplies. She would hostess the game tonight, serving drinks, emptying ashtrays, and being congenial. Nick could have had one of his crewmen do the duty, but Lara was a natural for catering to a man's whims. Anna only hoped she wouldn't get ignored by the flirtatious blonde.

Mitch hadn't followed the rest of them into the salon, and Anna had seen him walking the decks with one of the crew. Apparently he was taking the grand tour. She couldn't fault him for that. If you'd never been on a yacht like Nick's, it was fascinating to see the layout, to see how a designer had managed to fit so much opulence and convenience into a limited space.

While Frank mixed himself a drink at the bar, Anna set the juice deck on the table with the other fresh decks. Frank wasn't in on the con. Any dealer they could have trusted wouldn't have been approved by Dumonde. The other decks were straight, but they all looked the same. They would be changing decks throughout the game, and her main concern was that the juice come up near the end. Nick was supposed to take care of that. She wasn't worried about Dumonde's wiping her out with the first set of cards. He was too smooth for that. He'd wait, bring the game along a while, before he got tricky.

Mitch came up behind her and lightly touched her on the arm. "Whose idea was it to have the game out here in the middle of the ocean?"

"Nick's," she replied, keeping her voice cool. "He likes to use the yacht."

"Well, I don't like it. Not at all."

"Afraid of the water?" she asked calmly, returning her attention to the cards.

"No, Anna. I'm sure the ship is seaworthy. Like you, I'm only afraid of the things I can't control or don't understand."

Her head snapped up, and she glared at him in anger and confusion. She wanted to shout at him, How dare you expect so much of me, see so much of me? Instead she turned away, giving him the cold shoulder, and concentrated on the grain of the wood in the table. Her hands gripped its polished edge. They weren't going to make it through this night, she thought defeatedly. It would be Mitch's own fault if she lost his ranch.

Nick entered the lounge, discreetly ignoring the tension surrounding them. "Lara is going to handle drinks and food tonight," he said to Mitch, "and Anna and I will pull down the con. So, Mitch, old buddy, that leaves you to stand around looking like either an innocent bystander or a mean s.o.b. Take your pick."

Innocent was right, Anna thought.

"I'll take the mean s.o.b.," Mitch said, his tone of voice just right for the part.

Sounds of another boat pulling up alongside distracted their attention.

"That must be Dumonde," Nick said. "He told me he had his own boat."

After a few minutes Dumonde and the two businessmen stepped into the lounge. Anna detected a flicker of surprise in Jacques Dumonde's eyes when he saw her, but he hid it immediately and walked toward her with an outstretched hand.

"Mademoiselle Lange." He kissed the back of her hand, his lips barely touching her skin. "I'm honored."

"Monsieur," she replied, pleased that her mere presence had been able to throw him off-guard for a second. It wasn't much, but from here on, every move counted.

He was dressed in a lightweight black suit, the kind whose sleeves you could push up for a fashionable look. Anna knew he wouldn't be pushing up the sleeves, and not just because he was wearing a long-sleeved white shirt beneath it. She also knew there would be extra pockets sewn into the inside of his jacket.

His eyes were dark, almost black, his skin tanned and starting to show creases from too much sun. Anna had heard he'd once been a gigolo. It was easy to believe, for he was still youthfully handsome even in his late forties. He had a well-cared-for appearance, slick and self-aware.

In contrast, the two businessmen looked overfed and bland. The only spots of color they sported were the loud plaids of their jackets. Dumonde really knew how to pick them.

He introduced the two men, Dan Carlton and Albert Mawson. Carlton seemed to be the aggressive one of the pair, and Anna worked at politely untangling her hand from his grip.

"Gentlemen? Shall we begin?" She smiled at each of them in turn as she settled into her chair.

Frank came out of the galley, laughing with Lara, and introduced himself around the table. He was new to the islands, fresh from Vegas, and his complexion was pasty, with beads of sweat already forming on his brow from the unaccustomed humidity.

The spare tire around his middle would probably be gone in a couple of months, Anna thought. In the half-naked society of the islands, people automatically became more aware of their bodies, and most tried to shape them up.

He set his drink on the table and let the players look over the decks. Albert Mawson didn't bother. Anna noted the fact and tucked it away for further reference. Dumonde took more time with the cards, checking the seals and passing each deck under his nose. A tremor of apprehension shot through her. She ignored it, concentrating on the decks as Carlton checked them, then passed them on to her. Soon she would know how good Larry Walters really was.

Nick handled the decks last and stacked them next to the dealer. Anna knew he was trying to position the juice. Tonight's familiar feeling of defeat edged into her mind. If that was the extent of Nick's plan it was going to be a long night. The only right thing so far was Dumonde's not catching the juice.

It was eight o'clock. Anna smiled her last smile of the evening. It was time for business. "The game is seven-card stud," she said. "No limits." She glanced around the table as she spoke, and noted Mawson flinch at the betting. She dismissed him for the rest of the night. He hadn't come to win, only not to lose.

Frank took the top deck and started to shuffle. He was smooth and experienced without being flashy. He passed the deck to Nick, on his right, and he cut it. The hole cards glided across the table. He called the third card. "Jack . . . trey . . . ten . . . a queen for the lady . . . deuce. Queen bets."

By midnight Anna was ahead. Most of her winnings came from Albert Mawson, who had dropped out after the last hand. Nick was even, Carlton was down, and Dumonde had taken a chunk out of everyone. Frank dealt the sixth card.

"Pair of tens bets."

Carlton was into his second pack of cigarettes, and took the time to light another before betting his hand. "Tens bet five thousand."

Anna figured he had a concealed ten, but she doubted if he had two. He'd been losing on his bluffs all night. She held a concealed pair of jacks, with another one up, and it was worth stringing him along.

"Five thousand and raise another two." She counted off the bills and threw them into the pot.

Nick had dropped after the fourth card, so the bet passed to Dumonde, who showed a pair of nines, ace high. He doubled the bet.

He must have paired the ace or better, Anna thought. Knowing Dumonde, probably better. Carlton stayed in. Anna didn't hesitate to meet the bet.

Seventh card down. Fourth jack to Anna. Not a flicker of emotion was in her eyes as she dropped the corner of the card.

A smile twisted Carlton's lips as he clenched his cigarette between his teeth. "Tens bet ten grand." He almost laughed out loud.

Anna gave him a cool look and counted out ten thousand dollars. "And I raise it another ten." She could afford the action; she was playing with Mawson's money. Next hand she'd be playing with Carlton's.

"The bet's at twenty thousand." Frank nodded to Dumonde.

She could almost hear Dumonde's mind clicking as he glanced over the cards showing on the table. He met each of their eyes in turn with his empty gaze as he folded his cards.

Carlton threw in his ten thousand and called. "Read 'em and weep." He chuckled, flipping over four tens and the ace of hearts. He automatically reached for the pot.

His hands hadn't even descended on the money before Dumonde grabbed his arm. "We haven't heard from the lady yet," he said in a deathly-quiet voice.

Carlton blanched, and Anna could tell from the whitening of his face how tightly Dumonde was gripping him. It was a bad turn for the game to take, but Carlton was in the wrong.

Then suddenly Mitch was stepping between her and Carlton. He gave her a broad wink and casually leaned over to pick up her glass.

Turning his attention to the others, he asked, "Anybody else for a fresh drink?"

Anna wanted to kiss him for so easily defusing the tension.

"Uh . . . sure," Carlton said, backing down as Dumonde released his arm. "A double Scotch."

"A good hand, Mr. Carlton," Anna said, "but

not good enough." She turned over her four jacks, and waited a moment before methodically stacking the bills piled in the middle of the table.

Anger seeped out of the big man's pores, and he swore viciously. In a violent action he ripped his cards in half and threw them on the floor.

"Dammit! I want a new deck," he demanded in a harsh voice, daring anyone to countermand him.

"Yes, sir," Frank said immediately, adding a much-needed note of civility. In one deft swoop he cleaned the offending cards off the table, tearing them before throwing them away.

Mitch returned with Anna's tonic and lime while Lara served the men. Anna barely noticed him. Her attention was focused on Frank as he picked the new deck. Juice. They were in.

Her heart speeded up. Nick had seen it too. Fortunately their quick interchange was missed by Dumonde. He was momentarily distracted by Lara's flirting as she leaned over him to set his wine on the table. They couldn't have planned it better if they'd tried.

Anna had been cool since the start of the game, but now her palms were dampening. The gentle wind that had been blowing all night had died, and Carlton's cigarette smoke had started settling around the table like a shroud. She watched the shuffle, uncomfortably aware of how easily she was reading the cards. It was as if they were all face up. Tension, smoke, and bad feelings were taking their toll, and she had to force herself to calm down, fighting the urge to get it over with and move out of there.

She was enough cash ahead that she played the first few hands without deliberately using her advantage, but it was impossible to ignore the marks completely. Dumonde hadn't won enough to be satisfied, and she was surprised at his lack of card maneuvering now that she could see his hole cards. To throw him off-guard, she let him take a big pot. They were both biding their time.

One A.M. Lines of strain were showing on Carlton's face and sweat was running into the creases of his cheeks. Anna didn't have a hair out of place. Her eyes were clear, her movements sharp and clean. Dumonde was equally at ease.

Finally the time came for her to make her move. Fifth card down she was high with three nines. Carlton and Dumonde at most were holding two pair each. What they didn't know was that half the cards they needed were concealed by one of the other players. Cheating definitely took some of the fun and most of the psychology out of the game. But she wasn't here for fun.

"Nines bet fifteen thousand," she said, her voice cool and calm. The pot was pushing a hundred grand. She needed a large bet to make her move on, and she knew both Dumonde and Carlton would stay in. Dumonde was working a possible flush with his pairs and Carlton was playing desperately, trying to recoup his losses.

Sixth card. The men's cards didn't pair up. She was still high, and now working her own possible flush. In an attempt to get Carlton out of the hand, she doubled her previous bet. "Nines bet thirty thousand."

Dumonde met her money, and while they waited for Carlton's decision Anna caught his eye. She lifted one winged brow and smiled. "Monsieur? Would you like to make this more interesting?"

Dumonde actually smiled back, chuckling from

deep in his throat. "*Oui*, mademoiselle. What did you have in mind?"

"A vacation somewhere—maybe Colorado."

In answer, he reached inside his jacket and pulled out the folded deed. He dropped it casually on the table, to the side of the main pot. "A lovely place, Colorado. Do you have something to match?"

"*Oui*, monsieur." She extended her hand behind her, and Mitch gave her his deed. It was his last chance to back out, but he put it in her hand without hesitating. Good luck, scout, she thought as she placed it on the table.

Dumonde's possible flush had died with the sixth card. Only one card could save his hand, the jack of diamonds. With Dumonde sitting to the left of the dealer, his chance for a full house would disappear with the first card, a four of clubs.

Carlton had been watching the byplay with growing irritation, his jaw working his cigarette to a pulp. He grabbed his glass with a meaty fist and tossed the Scotch down in one gulp.

"I'm still in this game," he snapped, throwing his money on the table.

Anna wished she could leave after this hand. Her instincts were telling her the game was going to get a lot nastier before Carlton gave up, but a winner couldn't walk away. She lowered her eyes and took a sip of her tonic. It was proving to be a long night.

If Nick had stayed in and been able to win the hand, Carlton would have been less resentful. Losing to another loser didn't taste quite as bad. As it was, only she and Dumonde were left to feel the heat of his anger, the two who had taken him for close to a hundred grand already.

Frank dealt the seventh cards, face down. Four

of clubs to Dumonde . . . five of spades to Carlton . . . queen of hearts to Anna. She kept her face expressionless as a cascade of relief washed through her. Playing the game, she lifted a corner of the queen.

"Nines bet twenty thousand," she said.

Dumonde answered with twenty thousand of his own. Then he paused for an instant before meeting her eyes and dropping another ten grand in the pot. His hand moved over his cards as he put the bills on the table. The movement was natural—the cards were in front of him and the pot was in the middle of the table—but Anna instantly sensed disaster.

She couldn't stop her eyes from widening, her breath from catching, or her stomach from twisting in a gut-wrenching cramp. The son of a bitch had done it to her. Under different circumstances she might have been impressed, even awed, by his smoothness. But all she felt now was fury. Anguish clouded her eyes as she stared at the jack of diamonds now held in his hand. The four of clubs was nowhere in sight.

Dumonde caught her reaction, and confusion momentarily wrinkled his brow. Then realization dawned. She couldn't have known what he'd done unless she'd marked the deck, unless she was cheating. He immediately checked his cards but obviously saw nothing. Anger hardened the lines of his face, but only for a second. Then he laughed, low and satisfied. "*Touché*, mademoiselle." His accent turned the insult into a caress. She wasn't any better than he.

Anna knew she'd exposed herself and wished with all of her might that she could control the starkness of her emotions, hide behind a wall of ice. She couldn't. Her heart broke with rage and desolation, and it as all she could do to keep from turning to Mitch.

Everyone was watching her. Mitch with wariness and bewilderment. Nick with a hint of warning. Frank with puzzlement. And Dumonde with smug complacency. No one was watching Carlton . . . until it was too late.

"Nobody move," he said with a growl. "This pot's mine." He shoved himself away from the table and pulled a derringer. "Albert, come over here and get this cash."

It was ridiculous, some detached part of Anna's mind realized, that huge man with a little, tiny gun. But Anna wasn't laughing. She wasn't even smiling. It was all she could do to keep breathing.

The hulking Albert hotfooted it over to the table, shoving Nick and Frank out of his way to get to the money. Carlton covered him from the other side. "I don't know what kind of game you're dealing here, but nobody cheats Dan Carlton. Not no faggot Frenchy"—he pointed the gun at Dumonde—"and not no high-class hooker." He swung the gun around and aimed it at Anna's heart.

Time froze. The black muzzle filled her vision, sending a trickle of fear down her spine to her knees.

Six

Anna calculated the odds. He wouldn't shoot. Her life was worth more than a hundred grand and a few acres of smelly ranch. He couldn't shoot.

Carlton gestured with the gun. "Back away from the table."

She felt Mitch's arm encircle her waist as she stood up. He pulled her to his side and eased in front of her. Dumonde also rose, slowly, reaching for the deeds.

"I said back off, Frenchy," Carlton snapped.

Dumonde was a gambler, though. He picked up the deeds, speaking quietly. "The side bet was between me and the lady."

"Take 'em and you're a dead man."

Dumonde must be slipping, Anna thought, watching him hesitate. She was reading Carlton loud and clear. For the first time tonight he was in control. His head was swelled with the power granted by the gun, and he wasn't about to relinquish it. With a vicious backhand he knocked Dumonde against the windows.

During the split second Carlton was distracted, Mitch made his move, following through on the arc of Carlton's arm. He threw his weight at the bigger man, shoving the gun hand against the starboard window. The window smashed, and shards of glass sprayed the floor, glistening with Carlton's blood. Carlton had a good fifty pounds on him, but Mitch was fast. Their hands no sooner met than Mitch kneed him, sharp and swift.

With an enraged howl, the big man was jerked by a spasm of pain to a crouch. Mitch reacted instantly, locking his hands together and bringing them down hard on the back of Carlton's neck. The loser lost again, slumping to a heap on the floor.

Nick and Frank had subdued Mawson, and Jason, a crewman, raced across the deck, coming to the rescue a moment too late. Lara screamed and burst into tears.

Anna was glued to the floor, silent and shaking. The brutal violence left a bitter taste in her mouth and knotted her insides with nausea. She watched Mitch with glazed eyes as he walked toward her, shaking his right hand, the one that had taken the brunt of his final blow.

"How are you doing, boss?" He smiled his crooked grin, then studied her face as he sucked on the edge of his palm. "I think I broke it," he continued, shifting his gaze to his hand. "Next time we do it your way—we hire professional muscle. I'm not cut out for this."

His eyes locked with hers again and his smile faded. "You're not doing too well, are you, boss?"

She couldn't say anything. She just kept looking at him with wide, shocked eyes.

"Come here, Anna," he whispered. He pulled her into his arms, wrapping her in his strength and rocking her gently. "It's okay to cry." He leaned his head back to see her face. "It's been a hell of a night."

Anna had no intention of crying, yet she could feel salty tears running down her cheeks. Mitch held her more tightly and caught the moistness with the fingers of one hand. The tender feel of his callused hand was her undoing. She cried in his arms. She buried her face in his worn-out tuxedo, clenching his shirt and holding on for dear life.

He crooned sweet nothings in her ear, talking her out of being afraid, whispering nonsense until she was giggling more than she was crying. The jokes weren't that funny. It was his delivery and the tickle of his mouth next to her ear—and the sheer relief of being safe in his arms—that reduced her to laughter. She snuggled closer.

"I hate to break up the party," Nick said, leaning on the table, "especially when you two are having such a good time. But some decisions have to be made, and I could use a little help."

Mitch pulled a handkerchief out of his pocket and handed it to her, then gave her a quick kiss on the tip of her nose. "Feeling better?"

She nodded, dabbing her cheeks. "Thanks."

"My pleasure." His hands did a slow sweep around her waist, his eyes full of mischief. "Helping damsels in distress could get to be one of the things I'm best at."

"Would that be before your second-best thing, or after your third-best?" She cocked her head to give him a wry look as she stuffed his hankie back in his pocket. "Or could it go right to the top of your list, surpassing even your mysterious best thing?"

He shrugged, a smile creasing his face. "Depends on the damsel. And Anna . . ." His voice lowered, and his eyes darkened to a rich brown. "There's nothing mysterious about what I do best. It comes straight from the heart—and I think you're pretty good at it too."

His words resonated through her, reaching deep inside her, all the way to the secrets hidden in her own heart. She turned away from his all-seeing gaze, once again afraid of carrying the burden of his dreams.

"Okay, Nick," she said. "Let's take care of this mess. How's Dumonde?" Her voice shook, but the tears had stopped.

"He'll live. He'll have a hell of a headache in the morning, but he'll live." Nick picked up the deeds and handed them to Mitch. "I think these belong to you."

Mitch tucked them inside his vest. "Thanks. I appreciate what you two did, and I'm sorry things got out of hand. If you ever need anything, call me."

This time a jolt of real panic went through Anna, and her gaze snapped back to Mitch. Was he simply going to take his ranch and walk away? Out of her life? Just like that?

Suddenly she knew she didn't want it to happen this way. She refused to analyze why, but Mitch Summers couldn't disappear into memories. Not yet. She also didn't know what she was going to do to change it.

Nick started arranging the cash, leaving the players' winnings in front of their respective chairs. "I think we should leave everyone with what they had on the table. Except for Carlton. His money can go to Dumonde for personal injury. He didn't have that much left anyway. How much did you win on the juice?"

"I tried not to use it except on the last hand," Anna said, helping him stack the money, "but to be fair I probably picked up an extra twenty thousand without trying." Her mind was on a more serious problem than what to do with a few thousand dollars, though. What was she going to do about Mitch Summers?

"We'll keep the twenty," Nick said. "For damages from the creep and for Dumonde for inviting him. What do you want to do with this?" He picked up the hundred grand or so in the last pot and let out a low whistle as he hefted the bulky cash in his hand.

Anna thought for a minute, discarding a number of possibilities before coming up with one she felt was fair. "Pay off the dealer and hostess. Reimburse Mitch for his traveling expenses. Make up your losses and give Jason a bonus. We'll donate the rest anonymously to charity." She met everyone's eyes. "Do we all agree?"

Nick looked at her as if she were crazy. So did Frank. "Maybe we should sleep on it," Nick said, voicing his skepticism.

"Nick," Anna drawled with a note of warning.

He met her gaze, lifting his brows questioningly. "Are you sure?"

"Positive."

"Okay, Anna. It's your show." Reluctance dripped from every word.

She glanced at Mitch waiting for his comment.

"It's your show, boss," he said.

She hadn't expected anything less.

They divided the money, and Nick delegated Jason to return Dumonde and his guests to shore in Dumonde's boat. He tossed Mitch the keys to his own boat and car. "Give these to Jason when you get to the marina. He'll come back in our boat and you can keep the car tonight." He handed Jason the derringer. "Keep this until they're off the boat. Then toss it overboard."

Finally, he turned to Lara. "I'll understand if you want to go home"—he smiled a rogue's smile, his deep blue eyes twinkling with promise—"but you're welcome to stay."

If anyone had offered odds, Anna would have bet her night's take on Nick. She had to be the only woman in the world who had ever said no to that smile. Lara didn't let her down.

The rest of them said their good nights and climbed into the speedboat. Frank's silence in the back of the boat attested to his nervousness. Anna was still badly shaken herself, and she concentrated on watching Mitch turn the boat in a tight arc toward the shoreline. She took some comfort from his presence even at a distance.

At Frank's request, they dropped him off at one of the casinos. Anna understood his needs; she didn't want to spend the rest of the night alone either. The reality of a crowd would help dispel the frightening scenes on the yacht. But she didn't want a whole crowd. One person would do. She glanced across the dark interior of the Mercedes at Mitch, and confusion filled her. What did she want from Mitch Summers? Not a one-night stand. Probably not a love affair. Boy scouts didn't have casual love affairs. Then, what? She didn't know. She needed time to figure it out, and she wasn't sure how much time she had.

They turned onto the quiet street where St. John's house was and Mitch eased down the circular, palm-sheltered drive. Time was running out. Anna fiddled with her sequined purse, trying to put her thoughts in order fast, not taking her eyes off Mitch.

Without a word he put the car in park, turned off the ignition, and set the brake. He gripped the wheel in both hands and stretched his arms, staring out the windshield before cocking his head to meet her eyes.

She searched his face through the darkness, trying to find the right words, a clue as to what she should say. Nothing came to her, and as the minutes passed she felt hope die. Then Mitch shrugged, expelled a heavy sigh, and got out of the car.

Anna fought the instinct to cover her face with her hands. Instead she watched in the side mirror as his lanky body in the rumpled tux crossed behind the car. He swung her door open, then reached in to take her hand and help her out.

Silently he walked her up the low stairs leading to the front door. With every step his fingers entwined more tightly with her own. No other part of their bodies was touching. When they got to the porch he released her hand and shoved his fists in his pockets, watching as she fumbled for her key.

She felt worse with each passing second. This was good-bye. The scout had what he'd come for, and she was determined not to make a scene. She took a deep breath, trying to get the key in the lock. As soon as it turned she would raise her head and flash him a winning smile, wish him luck . . . and say good-bye. The tumblers rolled, and in the silence they sounded like thunder to her.

Before she could push the door open, Mitch's hand descended on hers, holding the door closed, keeping them in darkness. Her heart started pounding, too loud for discretion. All her senses were focused on the warmth of the hand holding hers.

His uneasiness was contagious, telegraphing itself to her through the stiffness of his body and the way he avoided her eyes. He rubbed his thumb across her palm and spoke hesitantly. "I'd like to stay with you tonight, Anna. Nothing else. Just stay with you so you're not alone."

She let out a heavy sigh and closed her eyes. "I'd like that," she whispered.

The sound of the phone ringing broke the awkward moment. Mitch pushed the door open and stepped aside so she could answer the call.

In a few steps she reached the phone in the kitchen, lifting it to her ear as she flipped the light switch. "Hello," she said, unclipping the sapphire earring. "Yes . . . yes, St. John."

Mitch followed her into the kitchen and she pointed to the wine rack, smiling. She was back in control. Mitch was still here. He pulled out a bottle and held it up for her inspection.

"No . . . I mean yes, St. John." She shook her head at Mitch, waving him to another bottle. He drew out a Cabernet Sauvignon, and she nodded. "That bad?" she said into the phone. Her face became serious. "Don't yell at me. I can't believe it either.

"Damn Dumonde. He should have known better. Yes, it fits. Tonight was a disaster, but I didn't expect anything like this." She paced the floor as she talked, ignoring Mitch and the glass of wine he offered.

"Isn't that overreacting a bit, St. John? . . . You can't be serious," she muttered, turning her back to the room. She listened for a minute, then twisted her neck to look over her shoulder at Mitch. Absently she extended her hand to take the wine. The Cabernet was rich and dry, filling her mouth with its soothing flavor. It was the first drink she'd had all night, and it didn't come a moment too soon.

"Yes," she said to St. John. "He'll stay with me until you get home. . . . No, I won't do that. We'll talk when you get here. Good-bye."

She hung up the phone, her fingers clutching the receiver as she took another swallow of wine. Then she looked at Mitch. There were a thousand questions in his eyes, but he waited for her to speak.

She thought about skirting the issue. What St. John had told her could work against her in two ways: Mitch could stay, out of a feeling of responsibility, or he could hightail it off the island. She didn't like either of those options. Her gaze roamed over the lean golden face and the unruly brown hair curling about his collar. No, she thought, discarding artifice with a slight shrug. That face deserved the unvarnished truth.

"We're in trouble, scout." She drained her wine and walked over to him to refill the glass. "Carlton is a bona fide bad guy, and he didn't like the way you busted him up, or the way I cleaned him out." She tilted her head back and met his eyes. "Where did you learn to fight dirty?"

He ignored her question. "How does St. John know all this?"

"It's a small island." So he didn't want to tell her, she thought, refiling the question for later. At least his broken nose didn't seem quite as incongruous now.

"What does St. John want you to do?" he asked.

"Go to our father's house until Carlton cools down."

"Where's that?"

"Miami . . . but I'm not going."

Mitch gazed at her, waiting for an explanation, and the longer he looked the more irritated she became. She wasn't going to tell him she wanted to stay as long as he did, and she certainly wasn't going to tell him about the family feud. She didn't quite understand the first reason to begin with, and as for the second . . . She glanced at his face. Well, a man who got along with a brother like Steve wouldn't understand the second reason.

She set her glass on the counter, deciding to ignore his unasked question as neatly as he had hers. "I'm going to change out of this dress. Help yourself to a snack." She started out of the kitchen, then stopped at the café doors, her hand resting on the louvered edge. She paused for a second before turning back around, feeling slightly ridiculous, but had to ask.

"Will you be here?"

"I'm not going anywhere, Anna," he said quietly, the warm reassurance in his eyes reaching across the kitchen.

She nodded once and left the room.

The dress would have to go to the cleaners, she thought as she stripped it off. The cold sweat of fear had dried on the expensive silk and left a clammy film on her skin. She stepped into the shower and let the hot water beat against her, but only for a minute. She soaped her face and held it under the spray, letting the water run into her mouth and hair.

After toweling herself off, she padded into her

bedroom and pulled fresh clothes out of the closet—an overlarge pale aqua shirt and matching light cotton pants with elastic at the waist and ankles.

A glass of wine, a quick shower, clean clothes, and still she felt nervous. St. John's revelations couldn't be so easily dismissed. Carlton was after her, after Mitch, and bent on revenge. She felt a moment's pity for Dumonde. He'd looked old and beaten lying on the floor, as if all his sins had finally caught up with him. She knew he was safe from Carlton. A con man always had a thousand places to hide until the heat was off.

The kitchen was dark when she left her room, but an art nouveau floor lamp in the living room was on. It shot a star pattern of illumination on the ceiling and dropped a more subdued circle of light over the couch.

Mitch was sitting in the middle of the couch, leaning over the table to pour another glass of wine. He glanced up as she walked into the room. The bottle hung from his hand as his gaze traveled from her bare feet to the damp hair curling around her face. He set the wine down and slowly rose to his feet.

She could drown in those eyes, Anna thought, her nervousness melting away under the languid heat of his gaze. Ever since his first kiss her body had been telling her something in no uncertain terms. She and this man could be magic.

The tux jacket was thrown over the back of the couch, the French-cuffed sleeves of his shirt rolled halfway up his forearms. He stood there, his arms hanging at his sides as if he were forcing them not to reach for her.

Then he broke the intangible contact by picking up the bottle and pouring the rest of the wine into her glass. "I'll get us another bottle," he said, stepping around her on his way to the kitchen.

Anna didn't understand. Something was wrong. It showed in the stiff impatience of his move- ments, the stark mask of his face. She sat down on the couch and curled up in a corner. Then she worked at getting just the right look of distraction on her face.

Mitch returned and sat back down in the mid- dle of the couch, closer to her than she'd ex- pected. "Will this one do?" he asked, lifting the new bottle for her inspection.

She nodded, wishing he would smile. He'd been awfully serious since they'd come off the yacht. Maybe he was frightened and upset too. No, that didn't fit. He'd kicked Carlton's ass and come away grinning, more concerned about her than about himself. Which reminded her . . . She leaned over and picked up his hand. "Are you hurt?"

"No," he said, pulling his hand away.

Now what? she wondered in exasperation. What was eating at him?

"Thanks for . . . uh, taking care of business," she said. "I'm not sure how it would have turned out if you hadn't been there. That was a pretty impressive set of moves you—"

"Dammit, Anna," he interrupted her. "Don't you understand? Your life was in danger tonight and it was my fault."

Oh, guilt, she thought, lifting one brow. That she could understand. "Look, Mitch. I'm a big girl. I make my own decisions. Taking risks is what I do."

His piercing gaze saw through her flippant re- sponse. "Not with your life," he said.

She couldn't very well argue that particular point.

"Nick didn't plan his party very well," he continued, agitation deepening the creases on the sides of his mouth. "Those men should have been frisked before he allowed them on his boat. And having the game out there in the first place was pure hotshot." Frustration was making his voice harsh. "The gun took him by surprise. None of you expected it."

"And you did?"

He shook his head. "No. If I had I wouldn't have let you go."

"Mitch." She almost reached for him again, but changed her mind. "I've had bad surprises before. This one turned out okay . . . except for Carlton's being very unhappy and wanting to do something about it."

"Great," he said in disgust, his hands tightening on his wineglass. "Now what do you do? Spend the rest of your life watching your back? I've tried it, Anna. It's a rotten way to live."

"What do you mean?"

"It doesn't matter," he said shortly. He pushed himself off the couch and paced behind the table. "Carlton can't do anything to me I can't do to him first—and worse. You . . ." He paused and looked down at her. "You're vulnerable. You don't know about men like Carlton."

The way his voice lowered in concern touched her heart, but she was still confused. "Wait a minute, scout. Back up to my original question. What do you know about watching your back and men like Carlton?"

This time she knew he wouldn't ignore her question. He was taking his time about answering, watching her with a mixture of wariness and appraisal, but he wouldn't ignore it. One thumb was hooked into a pocket, and the other hand was running through his hair, sweeping it off his face as he looked at her out of the corner of his eye.

"I was a cop, Anna. San Francisco, Chinatown. I was washed up, burned out. I couldn't take it. No-guts Summers." He stared at her, waiting for a reaction.

She didn't respond, or at least didn't condemn him, which she felt he expected her to do. Instead she leaned forward and rested her chin in her hand, fixing him with a quizzical look. "Is that how you broke your nose?"

Anger flickered through his brown eyes, and his mouth hardened. She understood. He'd just spilled a deep, dark secret, and he didn't think she was taking him seriously. On the contrary, she was taking him very seriously. She just didn't think there was anything for him to be ashamed about. Pieces were falling into place, and she wanted to know more.

"That and a few other parts of my anatomy," he answered.

"I never would have pegged you for a cop. How did you end up chasing bad guys?"

"We're getting off the point. . . ."

"I want to know."

He eyed her speculatively, then dropped into a chair with a weary sigh. "Life-story time, huh?"

"Why not? We've got all night, or what's left of it," she added, noticing the pale light of dawn breaking up the darkness. She wished he'd come back to the couch, but she wasn't going to push her luck.

"Law and order is a Summers tradition. Dad was the best beat cop Frisco ever saw. It didn't get him anywhere except an early grave, but damn, he was good. So the sons follow in the father's footsteps. . . ."

"Is that like the code of the West?"

He smiled, finally giving her the crooked grin she'd been missing. "Kinda, but Steve decided on living long and prosperously. He went to law school. I didn't have the ambition for it. So I ended up on the streets, wondering what the hell I was doing out there." He paused and the smile faded. "I could handle being scared. Everybody's scared except the fools. But I couldn't handle the futility. No matter how good I was, there were always more of them. On every corner, in every alley, up in the penthouses and downtown in the office buildings. I was doing what everyone expected me to do, and it left me empty." Memories glazed the soft brown eyes, and he shook his head. "Anna, I knew somewhere there had to be a life that was better for me than the one I'd chosen."

She dropped her gaze and reached for her wine. "I know what you mean," she said, and immediately regretted her comment. She hoped he wouldn't demand an elaboration. Comparing her minor dissatisfactions with what he must have gone through seemed ridiculous. She changed the subject. "What do you do in Colorado?"

"I teach skiing in the winter and guide fishermen the rest of the year, and I'm pretty good at it. Steve and I split the profits from leasing our fishing rights. You'll get a part of those now from your riverfront acreage."

She smiled and winked. "Income property, just what I needed to round out my portfolio."

"What do you want from life, Anna?"

So, he wasn't going to let it slide, she thought, cringing inwardly.

"Our positions are hardly comparable. I like what I do and"— she cocked her head—"I'm very good at it. It's just that lately I've been feeling as if there should be . . . I don't know . . . more, I guess." She wouldn't blame him if he dismissed her problem as negligible.

But a responsive gleam in his eyes told her he wouldn't. "Yeah. I've been feeling a few pieces are missing myself," he said, gazing at her with an intensity that went right to her core. Sooner or later she'd learn not to underestimate him.

If he'd been sitting next to her, she would have reached out and trailed her fingers across the worry lines etched into his face, smoothing them away, easing the seriousness back into a smile—or soothing it with a kiss. He knew it too. She could tell by the way he was watching her, searching her face with an almost tangible caress. He focused on her mouth, then sighed as he met her eyes.

Tension flowed between them, heightening their awareness of every nuance of movement and emotion. Anticipation hung in the air, heavy and sparked with excitement. Anna's mouth went dry, and she wanted his tongue to wet her lips—tasting, giving, taking.

Imagining his kiss, the feel of him in her arms, caused her to catch her breath with wanting. But she was afraid to move, afraid of breaking the sensual spell weaving around and through them.

"Don't go to Miami, Anna," he whispered. "Come with me."

His request left her speechless. Her lips parted slightly as she stared across the room at him. She hadn't expected anything like this, and she wasn't sure what prompted his offer: protectiveness or desire. He could fulfill her need for protection and satisfy her longing, but what did he want?

Before she had time to think, let alone formulate an answer, he spoke again, cooling the emotional impact of his first words.

"Miami is too close to Nassau. For all we know, Carlton could be based in Miami. I'd like time to check him out and I'd feel a lot better if you were where I could keep an eye on you. I'm responsible for this situation, and despite what some people may think, I don't take my responsibilities lightly. With luck I can get a handle on Carlton in a few weeks." His gaze shifted to the floor and he leaned forward, resting his chin on his twined fingers. "Then you can leave . . . if you want to."

The last words were barely a whisper, and Anna wasn't sure if she'd heard them or if she'd said them to herself.

"You didn't seem too hot on going to Miami anyway," he continued, "and you've got a home in Colorado now, your own place. The acreage comes complete with a cabin. It's not what you're used to, and you're welcome to stay in the main house, but—" He cut his rambling short, dropping his hands between his knees and slowly raising his head to meet her eyes.

"What I'm trying to say is, we both know there's something special going on here, Anna, but there are no strings attached to the offer."

No strings? Was he crazy? Her emotions were strung out in a hundred directions between wanting him and apprehension. She hadn't taken St. John's warnings to heart, but Mitch obviously considered them very serious. That alone was enough to unnerve her. Personal violence was outside her realm of experience, and she didn't want to deal with it now. She wanted to laugh off his fears for her safety, tell him he was blowing it out of proportion, go back a week in time, and never meet Mitch Summers.

No. She pulled her thoughts to a screeching halt. She'd still want to meet Mitch, still want the kiss under the shower. Out of frustration and fear, she got angry. She paced around the room, arms flailing.

"I don't like being backed in a corner, Mitch. I don't like it at all." She turned on him. "What the hell was your brother—a lawyer, for crying out loud—thinking?"

"Your involvement is my fault, Anna. Not his." Mitch's voice was cool, his eyes unwavering.

"I don't need this," she snapped, resenting how easily he shouldered all the responsibility. "Take your ranch and we'll call it even. I don't need any of it. I don't need you." The angry words were out before she thought, but she couldn't pull them back. A real pain tightened in her chest as she watched his face harden in an act of survival. *Touché*, Lange, she thought. You finally got him to throw up a barrier—against you.

"Dammit," she muttered, turning on her heel and stomping out of the room.

She slammed her bedroom door behind her and immediately felt like a fool. What was happening to her? Her not completely dissatisfying life was crumbling around her ears and there wasn't a thing she could do about it. If she was in danger, this was not the time for childish reactions.

She slowed her breathing and listened for the inevitable shutting of the front door. When it came

she winced, hating herself for being such an id-
iot. Ten minutes ago she couldn't have imagined
throwing Mitch Summers away. More than anything she'd wanted to be closer to him. He'd shared
something important, offered his help, and she'd
slapped him in the face with it. Damn.

She'd give him fifteen minutes and then call his
hotel. He was right. She had no business hanging
around Nassau waiting for Carlton to make a move.
The odds weren't in her favor.

The sound of voices penetrated her thoughts.
Angry voices. So he hadn't left. She listened closer.
St. John had arrived. Her hand reached for the
doorknob just as someone knocked.

She opened the door and looked up at Mitch.
His face was expressionless, without a hint of the
softness she remembered in the brown eyes. It
hurt to think she'd put the blankness there. One
of his grins was worth a thousand false smiles,
and she wished she had a magic word to bring it
back.

She'd never thought she'd make a fool of herself
over a man again, but maybe now was the time
to take a chance.

She opened the door a little wider, reached for
his hand, and pulled him into her room. She
didn't want St. John to witness what she had to
say. Mitch hesitated, but she'd already decided on
her course of action—and it started with an apol-
ogy. Her courage was bolstered by knowing that
Mitch, of all men, would be the least likely to
throw it back in her face.

The room was dark, and she was thankful he
couldn't see the myriad emotions crossing her
face as she struggled for a beginning.

"Mitch . . ."

"Anna . . ."

They both spoke at once, but Anna was determined to say her piece, to give him the upper hand.

"I'm sorry. You're right. It's stupid for me to stay in Nassau. There are a hundred places I can go besides Miami. I just want you to know that I don't hold you responsible." Her voice trailed off as he dropped her hand and stepped back, turning away from her.

His voice was a husky whisper in the darkness. "Don't do this to me, Anna."

She could barely make out the dim outline of his back, his shoulders hunched, his arms stiff, and his hands shoved into his pockets.

"Don't run away," he said, "I can understand why you wouldn't want to go to the ranch. You'd probably go crazy stuck in a dump like Hot Sulphur Springs. But if you want to go to Monte Carlo or Paris, all I ask is that you let me come with you until we know whether Carlton can do any damage."

He turned back around, and even in the darkness she felt the intensity of his gaze. "I'd go crazy wondering if you were safe."

On the outside Anna marveled at his boundless capacity for opening himself up, leaving himself an easy mark for rejection. On the inside her heart warmed at his concern. And, she had to admit, she hadn't turned him down yet.

She needed one more piece to pull this puzzle together, and she was tempted to turn on the light just so she could watch his reaction to her next words.

"You care about me, don't you, Mitch?"

"I haven't made any secret about that," he murmured, cupping her chin in his rough hand.

She stood perfectly still under his gentle caress, touched on a level deeper than physical sensuality. "I'm not talking about attraction. I mean caring." She wished desperately that she could see his face. She was taking a chance, pushing him like this, and her heart started to pound as she waited for his reply.

In answer he brought his other hand up to her cheek, holding her face and running his thumbs across her satiny skin. "That's what I'm best at, Anna. And since I met you, I've been getting better all the time."

The quiet interlude was broken by a sharp rap on the door. St. John. She'd forgotten about St. John. Mitch seemed to have that effect on her, making her forget about the rest of the world.

"Anna," St. John said, his voice cutting through the door," "I need to see you. There isn't much time."

As she reached for the doorknob Mitch bent his head and stole a kiss, tantalizing her with the swift caress of his tongue over her lips. "Whatever you decide, Anna," he said, "please include me in your life for a few weeks."

It was a straightforward request—no pleading, no coercion. She opened the door, and he stepped away from her.

St. John was angry. Eyes didn't really shoot flames and ears didn't smoke, but he was doing a pretty good imitation. He grabbed Anna's arm and jerked her to his side, leveling a dangerous stare at Mitch. "You," he said through clenched teeth, "should be drawn, quartered, and hung out to dry."

Threat and violence arced between the two men, and Anna didn't know whom she feared for the most. St. John was bigger, but Mitch had already proven how meaningless that was in a fight. Heaven forbid he should do to St. John what he'd done to Carlton.

It was up to her to defuse the situation, fast. She wrapped an arm around St. John's waist and started walking toward the living room, away from Mitch.

"Get the hell out of my house." St. John threw the words over his shoulder.

Mitch's eyes snapped to Anna's, silently asking her for a decision. Tension carved his face into harsh angles.

She was torn, but if she let him leave like this, it would be good-bye. She couldn't take the chance. "Don't go, Mitch," she said.

St. John's muscles instantly tightened under her arm. He gazed down at her with stormy gray eyes, searching for a reason she was incapable of giving him. St. John would have to trust her on this one. She'd have to trust herself.

He reached into his pocket and pulled out a plane ticket. "I bought you a ticket on Chalk's next flight out of here to Miami. You're going to be on it. I called Dad; he'll be at the airport." He ignored Mitch, focusing all his attention on Anna.

She drew the ticket out of his hand, glancing back at Mitch. "We need another one—and two connections to Denver." The dice were cast. She'd have to play them as they lay.

"Anna," St. John whispered harshly, pulling her around and placing himself between her and Mitch. "You can't be serious."

St. John had never been angry with her before,

not like this, and it shook her confidence. She tried to explain. "I won't go to Miami with my tail between my legs. I own part of a ranch in Colorado with my own house on it. No one will look for me there. St. John,"—she emphasized his name by lowering her voice—"*I* wouldn't even look for me there."

"You got that right," he snapped, then changed his tactics from anger to concern. "I didn't tell Dad the particulars. He loves you, Anna. He won't make it hard for you to be home. He's worried. Doesn't he deserve some consideration?"

"Cheap shot, St. John."

"Truth, babe."

"I'm going to Denver," she said with a calm authority she was far from feeling.

St. John's eyes pleaded with her, his hands gripping her shoulders. Finally, at her lack of response, he gave up and turned on Mitch with the remainder of his pent-up animosity. "Does this ranch have a phone?"

Mitch nodded.

"Then write down the number, along with the name of your brother's law firm," St. John demanded, jabbing a finger at the desk pad next to the phone. "And I want directions to your place."

When Mitch was finished, St. John ripped the page off the pad. "Now, Mr. Summers, listen to this. Anything happens to my sister and you have no place to hide. And when I'm finished with you, your brother loses his job, his license. He'll never work in the States again." He glanced down at the paper clenched in his fist. "Well, you got the law firm right. The rest of this had better check out."

Mitch's face was passive, his body relaxed, as he listened to St. John's threats. If anything he was the calmest one in the room. Then suddenly Anna remembered the scene on the yacht. Surprise had given Mitch his edge. No one looking at that face would expect danger.

He moved, and she caught her breath, a shaft of panic cutting through her insides. But he only reached for his jacket on the back of the couch. Pulling out the deeds, he shot her a quick glance and smiled, the crooked grin that always fought with his nose.

He handed the deeds to St. John. "Collateral," he said. "And, Mr. Lange . . . before anything happens to Anna, they'll have to get through me."

St. John gave him a disgusted look, summing up his appraisal of Mitch Summers with one deprecating sneer.

Mitch only smiled more widely.

Seven

Black asphalt raced under the Speedster. They wound their way up I-70 through the mountains, the wind roaring in their ears, Mitch wrapping the gears all the way.

Their reception in Miami had been cold, with James Lange echoing St. John's sentiments exactly. His welcoming smile had faded fast when he realized what Anna was going to do, where she was going to go—what she had already done. He hadn't tried to dissuade her, though, knowing his bridges had been burned on that avenue a long time ago. Parting words between father and daughter had been kept to a minimum, with only the slightest fragment of a deeper love showing through.

Denver had been different. In Denver she had stepped into Mitch's world—brighter sunshine, bluer skies, and his infectious enthusiasm lighting everything within a fifty-yard radius.

He'd hustled her up the concourse, taken the escalator steps two at a time down to the baggage-claim area, grabbed their luggage, and hailed a cab—all in a record-breaking twenty minutes. Anna had never gotten her luggage in under half an hour in her life, and that had been on an island hop.

When the cab headed away from the jagged mountains to the west, Mitch explained that they were going to pick up his car at a friend's house. The taxi stopped in front of a two-story town house, lushly landscaped with river rock and evergreens. A bright red Porsche was parked on the street. Anna didn't think anybody ever parked a Porsche on the street, not when there was a perfectly good single-car garage attached to the house.

Mitch knocked once on the door and opened it. A petite blonde peaked around a corner farther down the hall, and a wide smile split her face when she saw him.

Yes, this was a lot different from their reception in Miami, Anna thought as she watched a warm greeting, full of hugs and kisses. A very warm greeting. She was about ready to go back outside and stop the cab, when Mitch turned and put his arm around her, drawing her close. Introductions were made. Her name was Mandy. Sweet, cute, bouncy Mandy. Mitch and Mandy. The thought almost made her gag.

"How is she?" Mitch asked Mandy.

For a second Anna thought he was soliciting an opinion about her. But no. Mandy plucked something off the wall behind him, then dangled a set of keys in front of him.

"I didn't even warm the engine," she said with a sly smile, "and we've had a couple of cold nights since you've been gone."

Anna knew that smile. She'd used it herself a few times. But under these circumstances, and directed at Mitch, it made her heartsick.

Mitch smiled the same smile back at Mandy

and lifted the keys out of her hand. "I'll warm her engine just fine, thank you, and I'll talk to David about warming yours, sweetheart."

Anna breathed an inward sigh of relief. David and Mandy she could handle. The sexual teasing was just that—teasing.

They trooped into the garage with their luggage, and when the light went on Anna let out a slow whistle.

Gleaming black, looking fast, the sports car hugged the floor. Half a windshield raked, baggy top, fancy wheels. A Speedster. She fell in love at first sight.

"Do you feel lucky?" Mitch asked her.

Lucky, light, and loving every minute of it, she thought. She couldn't wait to snuggle into one of those leather bucket seats. "How lucky do I need to feel?" she replied.

"Lucky enough to hold back the rain and snow for two hours."

"No problem, scout." She inched her way around the car, one hand rubbing the sleek, dark curves.

When they were roaring down the block—Speedsters roar even in first gear, Anna discovered—she turned to Mitch and said, "You and Mandy . . . and David must be awfully close friends."

"David and I worked on the force together in San Francisco, but what makes you say that?"

"They parked their Porsche on the street and let you have their garage."

He turned to face her, and a grin spread over his face and lit his eyes. "Ah, honey." He sighed. "But I've got the Speedster."

With the luggage tied down on the diminutive space behind the seats, they couldn't put the top up. Wind and noise created a maelstrom of excitement as they screamed down Floyd Hill, practically airborne on the wide, sweeping curves.

Rock and roll pounded out a heavy rhythm under the roar of the engine. Mitch had outfitted Anna with a portable cassette player, using the headphones to anchor a large-brimmed navy ball cap to her head. SPEED SKIING was written in bright yellow letters on the cap, and after this ride Anna felt ready to take it on, willing to bet that Mitch had done it and loved it. He looked like a racer in his worn leather jacket and aviator shades, his hair blowing in the wind.

Having fun was turning out to be another one of the things Mitch did best. She put it on the list she was keeping for him—right up there with his kisses.

He handled the oversteer with true finesse, especially on the exits. The Granby sign was a flash of green as they zoomed by. He banked for the outside, flicked the wheel, the rear end slid into place, and they tore up the ramp. Anna loved it. This was definitely fast-track action.

Berthoud Pass was another story. She clutched the dash, her knuckles white, bracing herself on every hairpin turn, forcing herself not to look at the drop-off cliffs speeding by, inches from the tires. She would have closed her eyes, but her stomach kept telling her not to chance it. People didn't invite friends back who threw up in their Speedsters.

The road leveled out as they pulled into Winter Park, and she watched the little towns fly by. They didn't fly by because of Mitch's speed—he was doing the limit—but because they were so little. Fraser, Tabernash, which she almost missed. Granby took a little longer.

On the western outskirts of Granby they crossed the Colorado River. Before the next bridge Mitch signaled for a left-hand turn and downshifted the Speedster onto a graveled road.

They roared and crept along half a mile next to the river. Cottonwoods fluttered a shower of golden leaves into the sports car. Late summer in Nassau was mid-fall in the Rocky Mountain high country. Sunlight dimmed as heavy blue clouds rolled in over the mountaintops and shadowed the meadows.

Mitch pulled up in front of an ancient weathered barn and jumped out to swing the doors open. He took a moment to let his gaze wander over the tranquil solitude of the ranch, stretching his body and breathing in the crisp, clean air. A smile of pure satisfaction lit his face.

Anna watched every move as if she were seeing him for the first time. Only it was better than the first time. Tight, button-fly jeans hung low on his hips, a real improvement over the worn-out tuxedo. One ragged-edged pocket peaked through a hole at the top of his right thigh. She wondered what had worn his pocket out and tried not to wonder how his muscled thigh would feel wrapped around her own.

The flush of fantasy warmed her cheeks and brought a smile to her face. Her gaze took in his untied tennis shoes, the white tongues pulled up and out, above the narrow legs of his jeans. Count on Mitch not to tie his shoes.

He breathed deeply and raised his arms above his head, pulling the knit sport shirt up to expose taut stomach muscles, the swirling dip of belly button, and a marked line of white where his tan ended. The fantasy continued with her mouth tracing that line, her soft breath warming his skin, her senses filled with his special scent. If this was a private performance, she was enjoying every minute of it.

The cracked brown leather jacket broadened his shoulders, making his waist and hips seem even narrower than they were. Fashion plate he wasn't. Sexy he was. She was going to have to weigh the odds very carefully in this game.

She decided she'd had all she could take and opened her door. As she stood on solid ground, her head started to spin. She slumped back against the door and moved a hand to cover her eyes. The action helped a little, but not enough. She slowly slid down the curved panel until she was sitting in the dirt. This girl had seen the best bodies on the Côte d' Azur, she thought. He couldn't have had that much of an effect on her. Impossible.

"Anna?" He was at her side, kneeling in the dust and touching her shoulder. "What's the matter?"

The feel of his hand steadied the world, and she reached up to take that hand, holding on while she stared at the ground and tried to get it in focus.

"I'm so dizzy," she whispered in an unsteady voice.

"It's okay, babe," he said, gently pushing her head between her knees. "It's the altitude. You'll be all right in a minute."

He sat down next to her and shrugged out of his jacket, then draped it over her shoulders. He nestled her under his arm and held her for a while before asking, "You ready to move into the house?"

With the solid strength of his arm wrapped

around her and the husky whisper of his voice in her ear, she was ready for a number of things, most of which she was too exhausted to attempt.

She nodded. He pulled her up and slipped his hand around her waist as he led her into the house.

Anna barely noticed the wide front porch or the pine-paneled great room he walked her across. When they got to the open stairs he lifted her into his arms and carried her up to the loft. She didn't bother to tell him it was unnecessary, that she could make it on her own. Having him hold her felt too good.

He carried her with surprising ease, his arms tight cables of muscle behind her back and under her knees, warm and secure. The soft leather of his jacket smelled nicely of Mitch and made a comforting pillow for her head. His neck pulsed with life under her hand. She let her thumb graze the scratchy surface of his jaw, and he turned his face into her hand, gently nipping her wandering fingers. With a burst of energy he bounded up the last few stairs two at a time.

In the loft he turned her in his arms, letting her body slide down the length of his as he nuzzled the tender skin behind her ear. His hands trailed down her sides and cupped her bottom, settling her closer into the contours of his hips. Streams of languor sparked with fire followed his touch, every place his body contacted hers. Mitch and the altitude were even more devastating on the second floor. It was more than she could handle.

"Mitch . . . stop. I can't . . ." She choked out the words between gasps for air.

His mouth halted its tantalizing track up her neck, coming to rest on her cheek. His breath was a soft chinook of desire blowing against her ear. "I'm sorry, Anna. I forgot—no strings." He gathered her in his arms and placed a tender kiss on her brow. "Welcome home."

She was too tired to explain her words. If she was too pooped out to kiss Mitch Summers, she certainly wasn't going to waste her energy by talking.

Still holding on to him, she looked around the loft, and finally found what she wanted. The big brass bed covered with a blue patterned quilt beckoned to her. An all-night poker game, jet lag, and the altitude were ganging up on her mental faculties and shutting them down one by one.

"I think I'll just take a nap," she mumbled, pushing away from him and stumbling toward the bed. "Wake me for dinner, please. I'm starved." Her head snuggled into the pillow and she stretched the Speedster cramps out of her back, legs, and arms. The bed was heaven. Heavy lids dropped over her eyes and her inner lights went out.

Anna woke to the soft light and crackling sounds of the fire in the moss-rock fireplace at the foot of the brass bed. Smells from the kitchen wafted over the loft balcony, stirring her stomach into action. She carefully eased herself onto the edge of the bed, checking for dizziness before she stood up. Her inner gyroscope seemed to have oriented itself. She tested the floor. It was solid.

Bacon? She took another sniff, and a happy smile turned up the corners of her mouth. Ummm, bacon. What time was it? She checked her watch. Eight-thirty. That was Nassau time, she realized, which would make it . . . She did some quick figuring in her head and decided it was either five-thirty or six-thirty in Colorado.

Day or night? was her next question. She looked out the window. No help there. The light was halfway between on and off, but she couldn't tell in which direction. On second glance she noticed the shadows were sharper, the air purer, with a hint of sparkle. She shook her head in amazement. Anna Lange was up at the crack of dawn. She'd seen lots of sunrises ending a late night, but to meet one head-on was a new experience. It felt great. She didn't plan to make a habit of it, but today it was great.

Her suitcases were stacked next to the bed, and she quickly grabbed her makeup bag and headed for the bathroom to take a shower. No such luck. There wasn't a shower.

A claw-footed, sweeping, curved bathtub was her only option, so she started the water full blast and went back to get her clothes. She didn't want to dawdle and miss a prime opportunity to see the first bloom of day in the mountains. Her mountains.

What to wear? It was probably cold out there, and she was on a ranch. Jeans. Everybody wore jeans in Colorado. She knew she had a pair of jeans in there somewhere, a hundred dollars' worth. Rummaging through the case, she finally found them, one pair of black designer jeans with silver studs down the seam of the left leg. She pulled out a white cotton quilted sweat shirt with silver satin inserts and a pair of silver-gray, squashed-suede boots.

The bathtub was almost full when she returned, and she shimmied out of her clothes and dunked herself in. In minutes she was tripping down the stairs. There weren't any signs of breakfast in the kitchen, so she checked the oven. Sure enough, a platter full of bacon and hashbrowns was keeping warm in there.

She poured a cup of coffee and looked out the front window. Mitch had company this morning, a teenage boy with long blond hair brushing the collar of his red down vest. They were sitting on the wheel wells of the back of a beat-up pickup, with a golden retriever stretched lazily along the open back end.

They were both peering into the bed of the truck, deep in conversation. Their voices didn't carry into the house, but she could see the rapt attention the boy was giving every word Mitch uttered. She couldn't tell what they were talking about until Mitch pulled a screwdriver out of his back pocket and lifted a ski into the air. As he made an adjustment on the binding, she tallied screwdrivers on her list of things that wore out Mitch's pockets.

She sipped her coffee, pausing for a minute just to feel good. Nassau and its problems were a thousand miles away. Mitch had said, "Welcome home," and that was exactly how she felt this morning, as if she were home—at least for a few days. The way she traveled, home never lasted more than a few days or weeks at a time. This place was exceeding her expectations already, though. She hadn't expected it to be quite so breathtakingly beautiful. To own part of this—yes, she reminded herself, part of this really belonged to you—had turned into a real bargain, instead of the sucker bet St. John had predicted.

The downstairs was a large living area, with the kitchen at one end. Hardwood floors were covered with a variety of Indian and traditional wool rugs and a hodgepodge of furniture. From the kitchen to the cozy family area tucked under the loft, everything from Early American to Danish was represented. Comfort, love, and color were the only solid themes running through the interior decoration. This was a home that had grown over the years. It hadn't been carefully thought out by a professional.

Pain stabbed her heart when she thought of Dumonde walking through these rooms. He didn't belong here. This was Mitch's home, and Anna sent up a silent prayer of thanks that she'd taken him on instead of listening to her common sense. Up until now, she hadn't truly realized how much he'd had to lose. She banished the fearful thought with a shake of her head and opened the front door.

Autumn air filled her lungs and touched her cheeks with color. She closed her eyes, leaning against the jamb and breathing deeply of the cool morning stillness. When she opened her eyes again to take a sip of coffee, she caught the stunned appraisal of the young boy. He was staring at her with the bluest eyes she'd ever seen, his mouth hanging open and the word *wow* rounding his lips.

Mitch was kneeling in the bed of the pickup with the skis and didn't notice he'd lost his audience until the long-legged teenager stepped over to him and jumped off the side of the truck.

Grinning cockily, the blond boy strutted up the walk, his gaze smoldering as it traveled up and down her body. He stepped to within inches of her and leaned his head against the jamb, just above her shoulder.

"Hi. I'm Peter," he said to her breasts, his voice low and sexy.

Anna stifled an amazed chuckle. He was coming on to her! Hot and heavy.

"I'm Anna." She held out her hand, sure he wouldn't miss it. It was even with her waist—just below her breasts.

"So tell me, Anna." He gazed into her eyes, and she saw heartbreaker written all over him. Pity the poor girls in Hot Sulphur Springs, she thought. "What are you doing Friday night?" He picked up her hand and laid it on his hip, moving in even closer.

She might have eight years on him, but he had a good six inches on her, and she felt a moment of very feminine panic at the predatory look in his eyes. Then she weighed her options. She could let him down easy, playing along, or let him down hard with a cup of hot coffee on his overheated vest.

She glanced at Mitch, who was grinning and shaking his head in the back of the pickup, and was tempted to play along with the boy wonder. The kid was pretty smooth for a teenager, and she wondered if Mitch had been teaching him more than just how to ski. Shyness wasn't anywhere on Mitch's list either.

"There's a good band in Granby this weekend," Peter continued, "or I could get Mitch to loan us his car and I'll take you to Denver."

The thought of Berthoud Pass with Peter at the wheel of the Speedster was enough to cause a real tremor of alarm. She decided to let him down easy. "I already have a date this Friday, thank you."

She could tell Peter was gearing up to ask her

for Saturday night, when she heard another set of feet creak across the wooden porch.

"Back off, hot dog. The lady's with me . . . every weekend." Mitch laughed, tousling the boy's hair. "She's out of your league anyway."

He removed Anna's hand from Peter's hip and tucked it around his own waist. His eyes met hers. "You're probably out of my league, too, but I've got more stamina than old Peter, here, and probably a few more tricks up my sleeve."

Anna didn't doubt it for a minute.

Breakfast talk revolved around an incomprehensible melange of ski jargon that left Anna eating silently. Torque index, flex pattern, and torsional stiffness didn't even sound like skiing to her.

Mitch had introduced the golden retriever as Cam, which was short for something. No one remembered whether that something was Cameron or Camelot; it had been forgotten over the years. Either way, he made a great foot warmer as long as she kept slipping him pieces of bacon from her plate.

"I bet you ski one-eighty-fives, maybe even one-nineties," Peter said to her while he helped himself to a third scoop of hashbrowns smothered in sour cream. "Stick with me, babe, and I can have you on two-hundreds by Christmas."

The statement was delivered like a combination compliment—come-on, but for the life of her Anna couldn't decipher the mystery of his words.

"I don't ski," she admitted with a confused frown.

Peter looked at her for a minute, almost sadly, then turned to Mitch. "What are you going to do with her all winter if she doesn't ski?"

"I'll think of something," Mitch drawled, grinning lazily.

His suggestive tone started an avalanche of images coursing through her mind, all of which added to the fantasy she'd been conjuring up since his first kiss. She redirected her attention to Peter and slipped Cam another tidbit of bacon.

"I'm only staying for a few days, a couple of weeks at the most. I'm sure I won't be here when the ski season opens."

Without looking, she knew Mitch's smile had disappeared. He scraped his chair away from the table. "I've got to make a phone call. Then I'll take you out to your property."

The coolness of his voice wasn't lost to her. She'd spoken the truth, though. She didn't know what else to do. No matter what was happening between her and Mitch, no matter how beautiful the mountains were, she knew in her heart his lifestyle couldn't be hers.

The phone was in the kitchen, and she picked up enough of Mitch's words to realize he was talking to Mandy's husband, Dave, about Carlton. The intrusion of Nassau's problems here in Colorado high country was an unwelcome reminder of the precarious position she'd gotten herself into. Despite Mitch's shouldering of all blame, Anna knew differently. Not only was it natural for her to take full responsibility for her actions, it was vital to her sense of control to do so. She had known even better than he what they were getting into, or so she'd thought at the time.

After breakfast, a much less interested Peter hopped into his truck and drove off. Apparently, not being able to ski was an insurmountable stumbling block in their relationship. Anna chuckled at the triviality of his reason for losing interest, but at his age it was understandable. Common goals and dreams were important in any relationship, even if sharing a liking for certain sports wasn't. And that brought her full circle back to Mitch.

She sipped her coffee while he did the dishes. He had declined her offer of help with a wry grin and a shake of his head. For a moment she had been tempted to dig in anyway, for something about his look made her feel he thought she was inadequate to tackle a pile of dirty dishes.

Still, domestic duties weren't what she did best. In her world, people hired maids to take care of the necessary but mundane tasks of keeping house. Her silent acceptance of his refusal was a subtle reminder of the differences in their lives, a difference she felt compelled to emphasize. Something special was happening between her and the lanky man standing at the kitchen counter with his sleeves rolled up and his arms elbow-deep in suds, but it couldn't be enough to overcome their differences. Her common sense wouldn't let it be enough, but then, common sense wasn't proving to be her strong suit when dealing with Mitch Summers.

She put her thoughts aside as he finished drying the last of the dishes and turned to face her.

"You'd better get a jacket before we go out to the property," he said, flipping the towel over his shoulder and leaning back against the counter. "The heater in the truck doesn't work. We'll come back for your stuff if you decide to stay out there."

Doubt was written all over his face, and Anna realized she much preferred his light teasing to the cynical countenance she was facing now. Cynicism was her forte, not Mitch's.

With a short whistle he directed Cam out the door. "We'll meet you in the truck," he said.

She watched as he shrugged into a denim jacket and settled a gray cowboy hat on his head before walking out the door. A mental rundown of the contents of her suitcase confirmed that she'd forgotten to bring a coat. Her normally efficient packing system must have gotten fouled up by the expediency of leaving Nassau. She wanted to blame Mitch. He was obviously angry with her, and in self-defense she held him responsible for her lack of appropriate outerwear.

His leather jacket hung on a hook by the door, and in a huff she decided it would do just fine. She slipped her arms into the sleeves, but when she tried to zip it up she discovered the zipper was broken. Typical, she thought, shaking her head as her anger dissipated. Untied shoes, holes in the pockets, and broken zippers. The man needed someone to look after him.

Mitch's truck looked even less reliable than Peter's. The teenager's had been merely beat-up. Mitch's must have been the last survivor of a stock-car derby. Every panel sported a dent and every dent supported a ring of rust. There wasn't a handle on the outside of the passenger door, and she waited as Mitch jimmied it from the inside.

The tightness of her jeans made it impossible to make the giant step up into the cab gracefully. She weighed her options and discarded the running jump as too risky. Climbing hand over fist was the best plan. With one hand gripping the dash and the other dug into the bench seat, she maneuvered the tip of a boot onto the floor of the cab. Her eyes were level with Mitch's thigh, and she was thankful she couldn't see the crooked grin that went with his low chuckle. She didn't know what in the hell a truck was doing this far off the ground to begin with. Talk about hotshot. She'd show him.

She braced herself for the launch that would land her in the frayed vinyl seat. As her left boot pushed off the ground, her right one slipped, wedging tightly into the corner between the floor and the door. She gasped and grabbed for Mitch's thigh. She sprawled across the seat, one leg dangling in the air, the other trapped in the corner. The situation was absurd, it was embarrassing, and Mitch's chuckle had turned into a full-blown laugh. His enjoyment burned her cheeks in a scarlet flush.

"I can't move my foot," she snapped, wishing she'd tried the running jump or another pair of pants.

"Hold on, sweetheart," Mitch crooned, scooting over and pulling her across his lap. He reached down and freed her boot.

She pushed herself up, and his arms slipped around her waist. With his help she found herself sitting in his lap, face-to-face with his crooked grin and twinkling brown eyes.

"Never been in a truck before, huh?"

She glared at him, refusing to answer his stupid question.

"I like your jacket," he continued, holding her firmly in his arms, not letting her wiggle away.

She gave him the most lethal stare, daring him to comment further.

"I like you, Anna." His voice lowered, along with his mouth, as he kissed the corner of her tightly drawn lips. "I'm glad you're here, even if it's only for a week."

The trail of kisses soothed away her embarrassment, softening her anger despite her best intentions, and when he returned to her mouth he found her lips slightly parted. He deepened the kiss, spreading his legs and letting her drop between his thighs. The intimate contact melted the last of her resistance as he pulled her tightly against him. She met the gentle searchings of his mouth with her own, slowly giving and taking, carefully exploring each level of awakened excitement. And with Mitch's kisses there were whole worlds to explore.

She broke off the kiss, laying her head on his shoulder as he wrapped her in his arms.

"What are you going to do with me, Anna Lange?" he whispered in her ear.

Anna was at a loss to answer his question, so she spoke the only truth she knew. "I don't know, scout."

Eight

The dirt road followed the river, winding under the cottonwoods. They were a quarter of a mile from the main house when Mitch pulled off the road and drove through a swath in the meadow. He stopped next to the first in a line of cabins stretched along the bank.

Quaint, Anna thought, her gaze taking in the rustic log cabin, with its rough-hewn porch. Dried stalks of wild flowers were tossed gently by the autumn breeze, giving the cabin an abandoned look. She swallowed her doubts and forced herself to give her new property a chance.

Mitch leaned across her and jimmied the door open before he jumped out his side of the pickup. His silence unnerved her. She knew he hadn't liked her answer to his question. She wasn't crazy about it herself. No one had ever accused her of being wishy-washy, but her feelings for Mitch denied all reason. They went beyond the lines of commitment she'd drawn for herself, and she was afraid to cross them.

He was unlike anyone she'd ever known. He didn't fit into her world and she didn't fit into his. She knew she wasn't naïve enough to believe that love conquers all, and she didn't want to start something she knew she'd have to end. That path led to heartache, a heavy price for a moment's passion, a few days of delusion.

She ticked off her logical points one by one, until he was standing by her door and she was looking straight at him. His smile was missing and his eyes were full of regretful acceptance. *Better to let me go now, scout,* she thought. *Before the glamour fades. Before your honesty finds me wanting.*

The truth hurt, but Anna knew it was for his own good. Mitch deserved someone natural and free, someone who could love his mountains as much as he did, someone to iron his shirts and fix his zippers, someone to wash his dishes. Anna couldn't measure up in his world. He had let her have control, hadn't pushed her, and she would play the game by her rules, making the best decisions for him . . . no matter how much it hurt. The fewer memories the better.

She plastered a false smile on her face and held onto his shoulder as she got out of the cab. "Looks a little worse for wear, doesn't it?" She gestured at the cabin, adding a lightness to her voice she was far from feeling.

"It keeps the rain out," he replied, dropping his hands from her waist and shoving them in his pockets.

She had an uneasy feeling that he'd read her mind, that once again he had seen right through her. She followed him to the door and waited while he fiddled with the padlock.

"I wouldn't think you'd get many burglars out here," she said in an attempt at idle conversation.

"It's not for burglars." He pulled the lock off and gave the door a kick, loosening it from the jamb. "It's to keep the bears out. Doesn't always work, but you do the best you can."

"Bears?" She cast a glance over her shoulder and sidled closer to him.

"Yeah, the damn bears." A definite note of danger ran through his words, and Anna knew it wasn't the bears he was angry with.

He stepped inside the cabin and immediately pushed open the red-and-white checkered curtains. "Pretty hokey, huh?" he said, giving them a flip.

"I think they're nice. They look—"

"I bet," he said with a sneer. "You could always have some silk ones imported from Paris."

"Mitch . . ." she pleaded.

"Maybe wall-to-wall carpeting, so your feet don't have to touch a cold floor in the morning, the way we mere mortals do. It looked as if St. John had a few hundred extra chandeliers hanging around. I'm sure he'd send you a couple. And this piece of junk . . ." He kicked the bed. "You could get yourself a real fancy one, with satin sheets." He faced her, and as storm clouds gathered in his eyes, his jaw tightened. "I don't know who in the hell you want to share it with, but it damn sure looks like it isn't me."

"I'm sorry, Mitch." The words were a whisper. Her arms hung limply at her sides.

"You're sorry? I'm the sorry one. One sorry son of a bitch. You hit me like a ton of bricks, lady. I thought you could be mine." He leveled a steely glare at her, his mouth twisting in a wry grimace. "I thought *you* could be mine. What a fool."

"Do you want me to leave?" she asked quietly,

hating the question, hating the pain knifing through her heart.

"Leave?" He stared at her long and hard, then slowly started walking toward her. "No, Anna. I don't want you to leave. I want you to stay." His voice softened with every step. "In my house, in my bed, in my arms." He reached out and ran his hand under her hair, pulling her head closer. "I want you forever. I want you today. I want you now. . . ." The last was whispered against her mouth.

His other hand slid under her shirt in a sweeping caress, seeking the swell of her breasts. His mouth covered hers with a burning need, slashing across her lips. An answering shaft of desire shot through her. If he hadn't touched her, if he hadn't kissed her, she could have walked away. Could have left with only the memories of what might have been.

His tongue plundered the sweet mystery of her mouth, running along the curve of her lips and thrusting into the farthest recesses, sending shock waves of passion coursing through her body. Every motion cried out for a response. Every movement was the act of a man with nothing left to lose. His thumb played across the peak of her breast, and she melted in his arms.

"Feel how much I love you," he murmured. He lifted her hand and rested it on his fiercely pounding heart, then slowly, ever so slowly, he pushed her hand farther down. His mouth nuzzled her neck, his husky voice whispered in her ear, as he held her hand against the tightening fly of his jeans. "Feel how much I want you."

She picked up his rhythm, completely drawn into the undertow of his love, his needs, his promise. His low groan mingled with her sigh, turning her into fire. Both of his hands slipped under her shirt, his fingers sliding inside the waistband of her jeans, releasing the snap, lowering the zipper, pushing them over her hips.

"Don't stop, Anna." He found her mouth again as she hesitated, showing her with his tongue the path their bodies would take. As her hand found the top button on his fly, the word *yes* echoed against her lips. She undid the last button, knowing there was no turning back. She would take the chance and pay the price. She wanted him, wanted desperately to share his love, if only for a day.

"Love me," she whispered, her mouth tracing the angle of his jaw, her breath blowing in his ear. "Love me, Mitch."

Her hands glided inside his jeans, releasing him to the fullness of her touch. He pressed against her before he lifted her arms around his neck and cupped her bottom, pulling her into the cradle of his hips.

"Oh, I'm going to love you, Anna." His eyes were languid with the heat of passion, darkened with desire. "I'm going to love you as you've never been loved before."

He pushed her sweat shirt up over her breasts, then lowered his mouth to one peak. He teased with his tongue, gently nipped with his teeth. She sank onto the bed as he guided her there, his mouth trailing lazily down the front of her body. He caressed the gentle swell of her breast, kneading the satiny skin before running his tongue down the curve of her hip and farther. An erotic stroke between her thighs was followed by another, and another . . . and another, until her every breath sent shudders of exquisite pleasure to the apex of her femininity.

He pulled off her boots and let his mouth follow the trail of her jeans as he tugged them down her silky legs. Moving back up her body, he settled his body between her legs, kissing the corner of her mouth and the nape of her neck.

Her hand slid inside his shirt and ran down his chest, releasing each pearly snap until his bare skin warmed her breasts. Rolling his shoulders, he slipped out of his shirt, then pulled her sweat shirt over her head.

Her hands tangled in his hair, pulling his mouth back to hers. She kissed him breathlessly, desperately, matching his need with her own. The scent and feel of him banished reality, took her to a place she'd never been. A thousand sensations came alive under his touch, each one deepening the ache of emptiness only he could fill.

He rocked against her, starting a primal rhythm pounding through her veins. "Look at me, Anna." His hands held each side of her face, his thumbs brushing across her brow.

She opened her eyes and drowned in the liquid heat of his gaze. "Mitch . . ." she gasped on a yearning sigh.

"Shh . . ." His finger trailed across her lips. Then he entered her, slowly, watching pleasure suffuse the delicate contours of her face. He dropped his head to her shoulder, his sandy-brown hair falling against her cheek as he expelled his breath in a heavy groan against her skin.

The sun climbed higher in the sky, pulling the shadows from the cabin the way his loving pulled the shadows from her heart. Muscles, hard to the feel yet soft to the touch, contracted beneath her exploring hands. Emotions swirled in an ever-increasing spiral of wonderment and discovery until they were both lost in this world and the universe rained on them in a shower of stars.

Sweet tenderness unlike any she'd ever known engulfed her as they trembled in each other's arms. A lazy smile of fulfillment curved her mouth. He responded with a crooked grin as her fingers traced the golden lines of his face.

"I love you. . . . Shh . . . Don't move," he whispered against her lips before burying his head in the curve of her neck.

She lay quietly, reveling in the warm pressure of his body, until his reason for remaining still became sensually clear. He filled her again, his movements slow and deliberate until she quickened to his touch and once again reached for the stars.

Afternoon bathed them in a gentle light, warming them with the sunshine streaming through the window. Anna refused to think, refused to regret the memories they'd made. This day would be cherished all her life.

A low chuckle rumbled across her shoulder where Mitch was kissing her.

"What's so funny?" She bent her head and playfully nipped his ear.

He rolled onto his back and pulled her on top of him, smiling mischievously. "Next time I take my jeans off first. I almost killed myself trying to get out of them in the heat of passion." He gnawed her jaw up to her ear. "Let's go home."

The words sounded a cold knell of reality in her heart. "Mitch . . ."

"I know, Anna." He continued kissing her ear.

"Don't be afraid of hurting me. I'm a big boy. I understand that making love, being in love, doesn't change the world. Not until you trust love—and you don't. Let's just take what we can."

Anna felt a disconcerting wave of *déjà vu*. He could read her mind, she was sure of it.

He cupped her face in his hands, raising her head so she would look into his eyes. "Okay, boss?"

"Okay, scout," she whispered.

"You want to go fishing?"

She laughed as she rolled off him and sat on the edge of the bed. She pulled on her jeans and gave him a sly look over her shoulder. "Is fishing another one of your best things?"

"No doubt about it. I'm the best." He sat up next to her and reached for his jeans.

That you are, Mitch, she thought, thinking of his care-filled lovemaking.

Anna finished wrapping the peanut butter sandwiches and grabbed a couple of pops out of the refrigerator. Her body was still glowing in the aftermath of Mitch's loving. It had been a long time since she'd felt so much like a woman. She wished it could last forever, but she wouldn't think about leaving today, not while she felt so good.

Banishing the taboo thoughts, she searched through the cupboards for a bag of chips and some cookies. Breakfast had been a lifetime ago. She packed everything in a grocery bag and headed out the front door.

Mitch was waiting for her on the tailgate of the pickup, sorting through tackle boxes and fishing rods. He looked like an advertisement for a fishing-supply company, and Anna couldn't stifle a giggle as she approached.

"What is all that stuff?" she asked, gesturing at the layers of paraphernalia hanging off his body.

"Well," he said as he slipped off the back of the truck, "you've got your basic Class A fishing vest, complete with fly patch, various and sundry pockets to hold your basic Class A tackle, D rings for pliers, scissors, and your handy-dandy whip-out floatant." He zinged the small container out and let it snap back against the vest.

She put her hand over her mouth, hiding a smile. "What's this?" she asked, pointing to a brass pen-shaped object curved over his pocket.

"That's my flashlight." He flipped the tiny light on and off.

"Cutest flashlight I've ever seen."

"Cute? This is all professional equipment, the cutting edge of fishing technology."

"I guess that's a net hanging down your back. Not the best place for it, I'd imagine," she said teasingly.

"Oh, yeah? Watch this." He rolled his shoulders and twitched his fingers, looking like an old-time gunslinger. Then he dropped to a crouch and whipped the net around from behind.

Anna burst into laughter as she jumped out of reach of his six-shooting net. "You're crazy."

He pulled himself up straight and swaggered over to her. "Crazy about you, ma'am," he drawled, tipping his cowboy hat back. "Crazy about those big gray eyes. Crazy about that so-sweet mouth, and getting real fond of this spot right here." His hands slipped beneath her shirt and over her breasts.

She leaned into his body, parting her lips as cascades of delight shimmered down her body.

The kiss tantalized her senses, reminding them of the other pleasures he could give.

"You still want to go fishing?" he asked in a husky voice, holding her in way that left no doubts about what he wanted to do.

"You're going to wear me out, boy scout, and I'll be good for nothing."

"Nothing but loving."

"Nothing but loving you," she corrected him, putting a few inches of distance between them. "I like these," she said, running her finger along the top of his thigh-high rubber boots.

"Hip-waders turn you on, huh? I'll have to remember that."

"I like the way they accentuate your . . . uh . . ."

He grinned. "Yeah. And my . . . uh . . . likes the way you do what you're doing."

"Uh-huh . . ." she murmured, her mouth against his throat. "So are we going fishing here, or what?"

"I vote for 'or what.' "

"But I'm the boss, and I vote for a little fishing. Okay?"

"Okay, boss." He released her and reached for the fishing rods. "You carry the lunch and I'll bring the gear."

She looked at him quizzically. "Don't we need to dig some worms or something?"

"We're not using worms." He slung a creel over his shoulder and picked up the tackle box.

"Great." She sighed in relief. "I thought I was going to have to do something awful with worms."

"We're using flies."

She blanched, her stomach doing a flip flop while her face turned white. "Oh, ugh. I couldn't, Mitch. I just couldn't. Squish those icky things on a hook?" Her hand fluttered to her throat. "I can't do it. No way. I don't even want to watch you do it."

A broad grin split his face. "Honey, where did you grow up?"

"Miami, and there are lots of flies there, and believe me, Mitch, I'm not going to touch one, let alone impale one on a fishing hook."

"Come on over here, darlin'." He turned back to the tailgate and opened his tackle box. "Trust me, you're going to love these flies. Prettiest things you've ever seen. Scout's honor."

She hesitated, frowning skeptically. Taking two steps forward, she peered over his shoulder, prepared for the worst.

The sight that met her eyes was far from the crawly mess she'd envisioned. Neatly arrayed in individual compartments was a variety of hooks with feathers and brightly colored threads wrapped around them.

She wrinkled her brow. "Those are flies?"

"Finest flies money can buy. I get a buck apiece for them. This one's an original." He picked up a fly with wiggly antennae on front and back. "I call it the Summers's Bitch Creek, best little old nymph there is."

"And you make these?"

"Keeps gas in the truck and gets me a discount at the sporting-goods store," he explained with obvious pride.

Anna felt a pang of sympathy even though she knew it was misplaced and would certainly be unwelcome. She couldn't imagine working for gas money by making artificial flies at a dollar a throw. She could probably buy the whole store with a good week's take at a poker table or with just the interest from a year's investments.

"They're beautiful, Mitch," she said, glad she had managed to voice an appropriate comment.

"And they're murder on the trout. Come on. Let's go catch some dinner."

Anna pushed her sympathy aside and worked on her enthusiasm as they headed down the dirt road. Mitch guided her along the river, revealing the hidden pools and riffles where he assured her the fish were waiting.

Patience, Anna decided, was another of Mitch's best things. He never seemed to run out of it, no matter how many times she tangled her line in an overhanging pine tree or snagged her fly in the underbrush. Despite his judgment, though, she and fishing couldn't seem to find a common ground. Finally she gave the fish a break and sat down on the bank to indulge in the pleasanter pastime of watching Mitch.

For the first time since she'd met him she felt she wasn't the focal point of his attention. Every graceful cast commanded and received his total concentration. Broken nose and all, he was beautiful. Knee-deep in the river, with sunshine catching the lean angles of his face, and his skilled hands playing the line out in easy sweeps, he was a sight to behold, a man in his element. And she was a woman out of hers, a small spot of sophisticated civilization amidst the miles of wilderness. Odds were, no other hundred-dollar pair of jeans had graced this particular stretch of riverbank. Being with Mitch was an escape from reality, a reality that sooner or later would draw her back to fast-paced casinos and a nomadic lifestyle. She would take this time, but she refused to fool herself with dreams of forever.

An incredulous smile curved her mouth when

she heard him talking to the fish, telling the undersized ones they were going to be fine as he let them go, telling the keepers how beautiful they were. *No,* she thought, *I've never known anyone quite like you, Mitch Summers, scout's honor.*

When the rosy hues of dusk layered over the landscape, Mitch climbed out of the river. He carried their dinner on a stringer, only two of the many rainbows he'd caught. Arm in arm, they walked through the sunset back to the ranch house.

The tantalizing aroma of pan-fried trout teased Anna's hunger as she set the table with Mitch's mismatched china. A piece of this, a piece of that, and she knew each one had a story to tell. For her wedding she had received twelve place settings of Limoges, but they had all been returned. She guessed there was a story to tell in that, too, and she wondered if she would ever tell Mitch, if there would be time for such confidences.

He came up behind her, placing a kiss on the back of her neck as he set the platter of fish on the table. "Sorry you got skunked today. We can try it again at dawn . . . unless you've got other plans."

She turned in his arms and returned his kiss. "I think I'm booked for sunrise."

"Yeah, I think so too," he drawled. "A lot of sunrises."

She hugged him, loving the strength of his back and the arms holding her close. "We'd better eat before the fish get cold."

"You're the boss," he said reluctantly.

During dinner they talked business, with Mitch explaining how the split worked on the fishing lease. When he asked if she wanted him to book her cabin for next season or if she'd be using it, a chilly silence descended. His question cut right to the quick of their tenuous relationship.

"Let's not talk about it now, scout. Remember, we're going to take what we can, no strings. Only loving for as long as it can last."

He reached for her hand across the table, caressing her fingers with his thumb. "I lied, Anna. I'm not going to let you go without a fight."

Rather than balk at his possessive intentions, Anna felt a surprising thrill, a dangerous relinquishing of her heart. Smiling inwardly, she pushed away from the table. She was easy prey for those soft brown eyes, and he knew it. Time to turn the tables, she thought.

"I'll do the dishes if you'll start a fire. And then" —she smiled brightly, too brightly to deceive anyone who knew her—"maybe we can play a few hands of cards."

"A few hands of cards, huh? You mean like Old Maid and Go Fish?" A skeptical twinkle lit his eyes.

She let her hips sway as she walked toward the sink, stopping only to give him a sultry look over her shoulder. "Pokah, honey," she said in her best Mae West imitation.

She had definitely gotten his attention with her husky voice and come-hither look. He tilted his chair back against the wall, his eyes darkening with appreciation as she continued her sashay to the kitchen.

"Sounds dangerous," he said.

"Strip . . . poker."

"Real dangerous." His voice rolled over her like molasses. "But then, I'm a dangerous kinda guy."

"I've seen you in action, scout. I think I can handle any danger you want to pass out."

"I don't know. You might want to bundle up a little. You've never seen me play when the stakes are this . . . attractive."

A confident laugh bubbled from her throat as she looked at him from beneath sooty lashes. "I'll take my chances."

She didn't doubt for a minute that she would take him for every stitch he had on and still be fully clothed. His sweet face couldn't hide a pair of twos, let alone a winning hand.

He walked up behind her, dropped their plates in the dishwater, and slid his hands around her waist. "Don't say I didn't warn you," he sang in her ear before striding over to the fireplace.

After the fire was going and the dishes were done, Mitch started a pot of coffee. Anna sat cross-legged on the Indian rug in front of the fireplace and began shuffling the cards. They felt like home in her hands as she flipped them through her fingers and rolled half a deck over the back of her hand.

"Trying to intimidate me?" Mitch asked, sitting down with the coffee cups.

"Just letting you know what you're in for, scout. How about a little seven-card stud?"

"Baseball?" he requested, stretching his legs out on either side of hers.

"Baseball it is," she said, secretly amused at his typical amateur's desire for wild cards. "But three up means meet the pot or drop. Okay?"

He scooted closer until his slightly bent knees were touching her crossed ones. "Can we play in the dark?"

She cocked her head and looked at him questioningly. "You mean 'night baseball?' "

"Yeah, the one where I get a free card with a four showing."

"Night baseball, scout, not 'in the dark.' Maybe *you'd* better bundle up a little, or this is going to be a pretty short night."

"The shorter the better. I figure once you get me down to my skivvies we'll get to the really good stuff." He again moved closer and nuzzled her neck.

Anna was practically shuffling in his lap and his breath was tickling the sensitive skin at her nape. "Is this your not-so-subtle method of watching my hand?" she asked, trying not to giggle. "I can barely shuffle."

"I wouldn't say that." Feather-light kisses trailed along her jaw. "I like the way you shuffle. Yeah . . . Can you do that again?"

She snatched the cards to her chest, a flush of desire rushing through her and flaming her cheeks. Never had a man been so sensitive to her touch, so openly responsive, so unafraid of showing his feelings for her. It excited and alarmed her, this magic he allowed her.

"I have one more request," he whispered into her ear, having covered almost every inch of her face with a kiss or a nibble in his travels. "Can we play wet?"

"Wet?" Her flush deepened. Wet? It sounded terribly erotic or kinky to her. Her imagination was having a heyday trying to figure out what he meant. "Wet?" she repeated, a trifle breathless from the forays of his tongue in her ear.

"Yeah, you know . . . the one where the queen of spades is wild. That gives us nine wild cards.

And counting you makes it ten. I'm feeling kinda wild tonight, too, so let's make it eleven wild cards." He uncrossed her legs and maneuvered them over his own, then wrapped his arms around her and slowly rolled onto his back, pulling her with him until he was flat on the floor and she straddled his hips.

His kisses never stopped, and Anna was delighted to be sprawled on top of him in front of the warming fire. She raised her head and brushed his sandy brown hair back off his forehead, allowing her own to fall forward between them.

"Night baseball in the rain," she said, "not 'wet in the dark.'" She kissed the corners of his mouth and felt his crooked grin curve his lips up.

"I liked 'wet in the dark.' Maybe we could play that after the poker game, huh?"

"You are incorrigible." She smiled as she slipped off him. "Now, stay on your side"—she drew an imaginary line across the rug—"and we'll get this show on the road."

Anna came through the first hand unscathed. Mitch lost both shoelaces, his belt, and his watch. Anna sized him up, took a quick inventory, and figured the game would be over in two more hands at the outside.

Halfway through the third game the phone rang. Bare-chested, missing both socks, and only wearing one shoe, Mitch got up and walked into the kitchen. Anna couldn't hear the conversation past the initial "hello," but she did notice the muscles in Mitch's arms tighten as he turned away from her. His head came up straight as he listened. Then he sighed heavily. Her intuition told her the phone call had something to do with Carlton.

Mitch hung up the phone, but didn't release it.

His back was to her, one hand on his hip, his head lowered. He shot her a quick glance over his shoulder, indecision flickering in his eyes.

She waited for him to say something. A wave of uneasiness coursed through her. "What is it, Mitch?"

"That was Dave. He had news about the mess in Nassau." He finally turned and faced her. His face was grim, the lines around his mouth tight.

"And?"

"I think you should stay awhile longer," he said curtly, avoiding her eyes. He reached above the sink for a half-empty bottle of Old Grand Dad and poured himself a shot. He lifted the bottle toward her, offering her one of the same. When she declined, he downed the shot and screwed the top back on.

His silence told her he didn't want to talk about it, and she decided to let the bad news wait until morning. She wouldn't let it ruin their evening. He was obviously upset, yet willing to carry this burden alone for a while, and tonight she would let him.

Feelings of security and being cared for followed in the wake of her decision. Just tonight she would relinquish control. Mitch would take care of her. She would trust him, trust his love.

"I called you, scout," she said. "Are you going to come over here and face the music?" She made her voice light, trying to recapture the easy mood the telephone had interrupted.

He leaned his hip on the counter and crossed his arms, letting his gaze roam over her face as a slow grin revealed his white teeth. It was a sexy smile, filled with mischief and promise, and Anna felt the heat of it all the way to her toes. He reached for his hat and settled it on his head before moseying back to the game.

"That's cheating, scout." An answering smile curved her mouth as she watched his lanky stride, somewhat uneven because of the one shoe she'd already won. The cowboy hat added a rakish air to his grin and delectably bare chest.

"In for a nickel, in for a dime," he replied cryptically. Then he dropped down on one knee and flipped over his hole cards. "Read 'em and weep," he said with a wink, showing two nines to match the one he had up.

"Not bad. Not bad at all, but I think this hand goes to the ladies and her gents." Anna turned over her cards. "Full house, scout. Pay up."

"What was the bet again?" he hedged.

"Well, honey. I'll tell you. I let you have all those cards for just the price of one ragged tennis shoe and those beat-up jeans. In other words, you just lost your pants, cowboy. But . . . if you like, I'm open for a loan. I could give you my shoes."

He eyed her long and hard, as though he were seriously considering her offer. But then he stood up and his hand went to the top button of his jeans, and Anna knew she was going to enjoy this show to the max.

"That's a mighty generous offer, ma'am," he drawled, undoing each button, taking his own sweet time, starting a riot with her senses. He kicked off his shoe, and his hands went to the top of his now-gaping jeans. "But never . . . ever . . . let it be said that a Summers welshed on a bet."

Nine

Warm, cuddled, and thoroughly loved was how Anna felt when the first stirrings of waking danced through her consciousness. She stretched deeper under the quilts and turned her face into the kisses being laid on her cheek. A contented sigh escaped her lips.

"Hungry?" Mitch asked, wrapping his arm around her waist and pulling her close.

"Famished," she murmured against the crook of his neck, her mouth warm on his collarbone.

"Me or breakfast?"

"Decisions, decisions," she cried in mock despair before opening her eyes. "Feed me, boy scout, or be responsible for the consequences."

"Pancakes or omelets?"

She groaned, snuggling closer as she closed her eyes to think, trying to gauge her appetite. "Butter and syrup?" she finally asked.

"The works. Steaming stacks of buttermilk pancakes dripping with butter and maple syrup," he whispered in her ear.

"Sold. I'll take mine in bed." She rolled over and buried her head in the pillow.

"I thought you were going to cook," he said teasingly.

"Try again, scout." Her voice was barely audible as she felt sleep sneaking over her again.

"I'll wake you up when I get back. Ski season starts next month, so I'm going to put in a few miles before breakfast. You sure you don't want to join me? Nothing works up an appetite like a brisk jog in the morning. . . . Well, almost nothing." He nibbled her shoulder.

"Sex maniac," she mumbled.

"Health nut," he corrected her, and patted her on the bottom before bouncing out of bed.

Anna heard him rustling around the room until sleep claimed her. Her next waking lacked the coziness of the first. The insistent ringing of the phone refused to be ignored. She let it ring awhile before she started counting, and at ten rings she made the sleep-shattering move to answer it. Grabbing Mitch's robe, she stumbled down the stairs and into the kitchen.

"Hello." She ran a hand over her face, trying to rub the sleep from her eyes and mind.

"Anna? Anna. Where have you been? I tried to call you all day yesterday."

"Hi, St. John. Fishing." She looked around the kitchen and saw steam rising from the coffee pot.

"What?"

She opened a cupboard and found a cup. "Fishing." She poured the coffee and took a first tentative sip. "Ummm. Heaven. Fishing, St. John. We were fishing."

"When are you coming home?"

"I don't know." She yawned, and pulled a chair closer to the phone. The legs scraped across the floor, causing her to flinch. "As soon as this thing with Carlton blows over, I'll start making plans to return . . . maybe." She settled into the chair and drew her legs up.

"What do you mean, 'maybe'?" St. John's voice lowered to a no-nonsense level.

Anna held the phone away from her ear and gave it an exasperated look before answering. "Mostly I mean, I might stay a little longer. It's beautiful here. I'm having a good time, and—"

"With that bum?" There was no denying the harsh condemnation in his tone.

"Mitch Summers is not a bum. Relax, St. John. I'm a big girl."

"I checked his financial status, Anna, and believe me the man is a bum. His annual gross couldn't keep you in champagne. His credit rating would make a paper boy blush."

"That's hardly news, big brother," she drawled, picking up on his feintly veiled innuendo and trying to keep her hackles down.

"All I'm asking is that you come home and think about things before you do anything."

"Like marry a pauper? Or get made a fool of again? One of those things, St. John?" Her voice rose in volume as well as pitch.

"I knew it! You're thinking of something crazy. You always go for the bums." Anna could almost see him slap his hand to his head. She set her jaw, gripped the receiver more tightly, and refused to answer.

"Anna, Anna, Anna."

"I'm not speaking to you, St. John."

"Fine. Just don't speak to me here in Nassau rather than in mortgage heaven, Colorado," he pleaded.

"I don't want to be in Nassau until it's safe."

"Then come on home. It's safe. Carlton turned himself in to the Drug Enforcement Agency a few hours after you left. I tried to have you paged at the Denver Airport. You could have gotten right back on the plane. Anna, you know I'm only thinking of what's best—"

"What?" she practically screeched into the phone. "DEA? Carlton? What's going on?"

"Come home, Anna." St. John sounded tired. "The only people threatened by Carlton are the dealers who gave him the money he lost to you. He was supposed to make a deal, and when he lost the money he ran to the police rather than face his partners. He'll sell out everybody and their mothers for police protection. If your boyfriend had any connections, he would have known this yesterday morning."

An unpleasant picture started forming in her half-awake mind, a picture of a boy scout's lies. She tried to think back to yesterday's phone calls. He hadn't said anything about either one of them. She had assumed a lot of things, but Mitch hadn't actually told her anything. Maybe he had counted on that. The thought ran in circles around her mind, whipping up her defense mechanisms.

"Carlton was a drug dealer?" she asked.

"More like a delivery boy. He was supposed to make the trade, but apparently thought he could double his money and still make the deal. He took a chance and lost . . . really lost. After you cleaned him out, the only thing he had to trade was information for protection. The big boys don't like it when people play around with their money. My guess is Carlton isn't going to last long, whether the police protect him or not."

"And you knew all this yesterday morning?"

"Just a few hours after you left, babe. I was too late to catch you in Miami, but I sure tried in Denver."

She pushed herself out of the chair and set her cup on the counter. Staring out the kitchen window, she took a deep breath and formulated her conclusion. The scout had lied to her. Hurt was a fleeting emotion, quickly replaced by anger.

"I'll be home tonight, St. John," she said calmly.

A moment's silence met her announcement. Then he asked, "Why the sudden change? Don't get me wrong—I'm pleased—but why?"

Anna and St. John had always played it straight with each other, and she wasn't going to let her pride get in the way of their special relationship. "I think Mitch knew yesterday morning, too, St. John, last night at the latest. I think he knew and deliberately left me in the dark."

"I'm sorry, Anna." His voice was sad, and she knew he understood the implications of Mitch's lying to her.

"Not half as sorry as I am." She shook her head and hardened her heart.

A sarcastic laugh met her ears. "I can't say I liked the guy, but I didn't really think he was cut from the same cloth as Antonio. . . ."

"Damn," she whispered more to herself than St. John.

". . . This Summers fellow didn't seem that shrewd."

"Well, you're right about that. He's not much of a gambler," she said, then added, "He sure played his cards wrong with this lady."

"Does it matter?"

She sighed and dropped her gaze to her half-empty coffee cup. "Yeah, bro'. It mattered this time. Damn."

"Do you want me to pick you up?" he asked softly.

"No, I'll take a cab. See you later." She hung up the phone and covered her face with her hands. The dream was over, and it hurt. But she hadn't expected anything else. She'd always known it would end, next week, next month, whenever. There was no true love. She'd learned that a long time ago.

"Then why do I feel betrayed?" she whispered to the empty kitchen. Because you thought boy scouts never lied. Because everything about him sent a different signal. Because you wanted to believe.

She had to get out of there. She grabbed the phone book, flipped to the yellow pages, and ran her finger down the "automobile" column. She found car rentals and dialed the first number listed. She had to bribe the guy to pick her up, and she promised him an extra twenty if he came within half an hour. No man was going to make a fool out of her again.

Her next call was to a travel agent. Booking an afternoon flight to Miami wasn't a problem, but there was no Nassau connection. She told the agent to get her to Miami. From there she could arrange her own flight to Nassau.

Action and the need for speed didn't leave her enough time to change her mind. She *wouldn't* change her mind—no matter how much she wanted to. Better to take control of her life. Better to put some distance between her heart and her mind. Between Mitch and reality. Between pain and emptiness. Only once did it occur to her that she was falling back on her trusted solution to any problem—running away.

When the rental car pulled up in front of the

ranch house, Anna was waiting on the porch with her luggage, watching the road for Mitch and half hoping he would show up, half praying he wouldn't. She'd left a note on the kitchen table, telling him the coast was clear and that she had decided to return to Nassau. It was a cheap shot, but she refused to feel guilty. After all, Mitch had pulled an even cheaper shot.

Gravel crunched under the tires as they drove through the ranch gate. She had kept one eye on the side mirror all the way down the drive, wondering what she'd do if Mitch came jogging into view. But she never had the opportunity to find out.

By the time she arrived in Miami, Anna was tired, hungry, and grungy. The agent in Granby had routed her through every podunk city in the Midwest. Nassau flights had stopped running until morning, leaving her with two options, a hotel or home.

Home. The word sounded good, yet foreign. It had been a long time, too long. Doubt had dogged her trail all the way from Colorado. During her layover in Cincinnati, she'd lost her anger and begun wondering if her behavior was rational or merely comfortable habit. Back on the run, she thought now. Always running from something— responsibility, love, home. Time to grow up, Anna, she told herself as she stopped at a pay phone and dug in her purse for a quarter.

The call was short. She declined her dad's offer to pick her up, and told him she'd take a taxi. She'd be home within half an hour. His silence told her he hadn't missed her use of the word *home*. Then he spoke.

"Fine, dear. I'll be waiting . . . at home. I love you."

"I love you, too, Dad."

A new bounce lifted her steps down the concourse. For the first time in years she felt as if she had a direction, and it was "toward," rather than "away from." If nothing else, Mitch had taught her the value of forgiveness. The more she thought about it, the more foolish she felt. Leaving this morning had been a mistake, the result of a childish tantrum. She had been so quick to condemn, and running was always too easy.

As the taxi drove through the wrought-iron gates to the Lange home, she decided to take another step "toward." She would call Mitch in the morning and at least give him an opportunity to explain his lies. Deep in her heart she knew why he'd done it. He'd told her he wouldn't let her go without a fight. But he'd chosen the wrong weapon.

James Lange was waiting in the doorway. Tall and graying, he was an older version of St. John. He greeted her with outstretched arms.

"Welcome home, Anna." His voice caught on her name as he wrapped her in a hug.

Together they walked into the house, both knowing tonight was a time for healing old wounds.

Three days later Anna still hadn't reached Mitch, and her confidence was dipping toward an all-time low. The only thing she knew for sure was that he wasn't hanging around the phone waiting to hear from her. And being without him had proved how important he'd become to her. She missed his crooked grin and broken nose, his soft brown eyes and easy laughter. Inactivity left her more time than she wanted to think about all the things she missed, so she said her sweet goodbyes to her father and caught a plane to Nassau.

Her heart wasn't broken yet, just starting to crack in the more tender places. She knew Mitch loved her, and if this aching emptiness meant anything, she would put her money on love. No matter what happened between her and Mitch, she wasn't running anymore. The price for running had gotten too high. She'd lost four years of having her father in her life by running. And three days of Mitch's love.

St. John's house was empty when she arrived. She dropped her suitcase in her bedroom and immediately went to the phone in the living room to try Mitch again. The phone cord twisted behind her back as she walked over to the patio doors and opened them, letting the slight breeze blow through the house. Her gaze found the outside shower, and a pang of remembrance burned through her heart. Maybe coming to Nassau had been a mistake. In Miami she'd only had to contend with her imagination. Here there were solid memories. A kiss, a smile, a touch. Everywhere she looked Mitch's presence called to her.

The phone rang on and on and no one answered. She felt a hint of desperation. What if she never got hold of him? Where was he? Whom else could she call?

Stephen, his brother. The name popped into her mind. She dialed the long-distance operator. Checking the time, she decided to try Stephen at his office, and waited impatiently for the call to go through. Why hadn't she thought of him before?

When his secretary answered the phone and Anna asked for Stephen Summers, she was informed he was in a meeting. "May I take a message?" the secretary asked coolly.

Anna wasn't in the mood to play cat and mouse with a secretary, so in her own cool voice she played a bluff. "Tell Mr. Summers that Ms. Lange is on the line from Nassau and I will hold."

A moment's silence greeted her pronouncement, then, "Anna Lange?"

"Yes," Anna replied firmly, not revealing her amazement that the secretary had heard of her.

"One moment, Ms. Lange. Mr. Summers has been expecting your call. Please hold." The secretary's voice had warmed considerably, almost as if she were afraid Anna might hang up.

When the phone clicked, Anna dropped her facade of composure and let astonishment slacken her face. Expecting her call? Fast on the heels of wonder came fear. What if something had happened to Mitch? Her mind raced over a dozen awful scenarios before Stephen picked up the phone.

"Ms. Lange?"

"Is Mitch okay?" The words came out a nervous question.

"You tell me, Ms. Lange. I haven't heard from him since your wonderful coup with the ranch. I thought you were both still in Colorado. I can't begin to tell you how grateful I am—"

"I did it for Mitch," she interrupted, cutting off his misplaced thank you. "How can I get in touch with him?"

"I assume you've tried the ranch."

"For three days, without any luck. Can you give me the name of anyone in Hot Sulphur I could call?"

"Not really. I don't spend much time there. It's actually Mitch's home, rather than mine."

"And don't you forget it," she snapped. Worry was making her voice harsher than she wanted, and she backed down. An antagonistic attitude wasn't going to get her anywhere. "I'm sorry, Mr. Summers. It's just that I'm concerned about Mitch."

"Mitch can take care of himself, Ms. Lange. I'm sure there's no cause for concern."

"Then why were you expecting my call?" she asked.

"Frankly, after you won the ranch back I figured you might want more of a reward, so to speak, than Mitch is in a position to offer. I don't know how you pulled it off with only his backing, and I doubt if you're in the habit of financing this sort of thing on your own."

Anna's back stiffened in a flash of anger. This pompous man had a lot of nerve and plenty to learn, and she was just the one to teach him his first lesson. "Frankly, Mr. Summers, I find your attitude disgusting. Mitch's terms were more than adequate, and he certainly didn't resort to using something that wasn't his to pay me off. If anything, he showed remarkable astuteness in his dealings with me. Which is more than I can say about his dealings with you. I highly recommended that he sue you for breech of contract."

She could almost feel Stephen Summers squirming under her tirade.

"My apologies," he said. "You're absolutely right, of course. But there wasn't a contract. His suit wouldn't have had a leg to stand on."

"That's not why he didn't pursue it," she informed him in a haughty tone.

"I know my brother, Ms. Lange. And I also know he saved me from a very sticky situation. But if you're not requesting further payment, I would say our biggest problem is how to contact Mitch."

She relaxed, trying to defuse her hostility. "Yes. That's why I called."

"Short of actually going to the ranch, I would recommend continuing your calls, and I will certainly have my secretary phone from here. You might try the ski area. The season starts soon, and the instructors should be showing up in the valley. If you could contact one of them, he might know where Mitch is."

Finally a clue. She sighed with relief. "What's the name of the ski area?"

"Winter Park Recreation Association. I have the number here."

He gave it to her, then continued. "As I said before, I don't think there's any reason to worry. Mitch spends a lot of time hiking around those mountains, so it's not unusual for him not to answer the phone."

"At three o'clock in the morning?" she asked doubtfully.

"You've been calling at three o'clock in the morning?" Stephen asked, incredulous.

"Yes," she admitted.

A long silence preceded his next, softly spoken question. "Are you in love with my brother, Ms. Lange?"

The question should have surprised her more than it did. The answer should have been harder to find than it was. But in that moment she knew beyond doubt. "Yes, Mr. Summers. I'm in love with Mitch. I love him very, very much."

Ten

Someone at the ski area told Anna how to locate another instructor, but the instructor couldn't help her find Mitch. Apparently, no one had seen him since he and Peter had missed an organizational meeting two days before. Panic was beginning to overwhelm her.

She hung up the phone, her hand lingering on the receiver in the hope that she'd come up with another idea.

She picked up the phone again to call St. John, then replaced it. She would have better luck if she went to the casino. Tracking down St. John while he was working would take more time than getting to Runner's Cay. Besides, she wasn't in the mood to be stuck on hold.

The question "Where was Mitch?" stayed in her mind all the way to Runner's Cay. She raced through the half-empty gambling rooms, headed for St. John's office. She knocked once, and when she didn't get an answer, used her key. Flipping on his desk lamp, she checked his calendar and found it empty of afternoon appointments. Then she caught sight of an envelope with her name on it lying on the suede blotter. Curious, she picked it up. There was no return address, and the postmark was three days old. A confused frown passed over her face. She'd talked to St. John last night. He hadn't mentioned any mail.

She used his sterling-silver letter opener and slit the top of the envelope. As she unfolded the piece of notebook paper, a mixture of excitement and fear coursed through her. No one but Mitch would use lined notebook paper. Only one sentence was scrawled across the middle of the page.

She read the words over and over, until tears spilled onto her cheeks and she couldn't see them any more. She didn't need to see them, for the single sentence was painfully easy to memorize— "Was it so easy to leave me?"

The image of Mitch writing those words twisted around her heart like a vise, and she whispered her answer to the lonely room. "No, scout."

Clutching the letter to her breast, she walked over to St. John's bar and poured herself a cognac. She stopped at the usual amount, then tipped the decanter to make it a double shot. Tears and liquor, she thought. What had become of her? A fine mess you've gotten yourself into, sophisticated lady. Sophisticated, lonely, heartbroken lady. Her options were fading faster than snow in June, and getting drunk was looking better and better.

She went back to the desk, settling into the wing chair and propping her feet on the windowsill behind the desk. It made a cozy, private corner for her to drown her sorrows in, her back to the room, the leather wings of the chair encompassing her body and hiding her from view.

She read Mitch's letter a dozen more times,

until she'd worked up an unhealthy amount of self-pity and self-disgust. Mixing the two in equal parts with the cognac started the tears rolling again. When she finished the first glass, she went back to the bar for a refill and decided just to put the decanter on the desk. That way she wouldn't have to interrupt her blue funk again.

Halfway through her second glass she decreed herself a miserable excuse for a grown-up woman. By her third glass she was crying for all the brokenhearted lovers in the world, past and present. Romeo and Juliet, absolutely tragic, she thought, sniffling, and dabbing at the moisture on her cheeks. Tristan and Isolde, so romantic. She sighed as a fresh wave of tears ran into the snifter raised to her lips. She could return to the ranch and tie a white hankie on the car antenna, the way Isolde had returned to Tristan with white sails on her ship.

She giggled at the ridiculous comparison. Then she hiccuped, and hiccuped again. Getting drunk had been a good idea. She didn't know why she'd never tried it before. She felt better and worse at the same time, but more detached, with the pain floating around her instead of hurting all the way through.

Yes, she would return to Hot Sulphur Springs with a white hankie fluttering from her antenna. Very impressive, she decided. Surely Mitch would forgive her then. She wished the hiccups would stop. They made it very difficult to cry romantically. Maybe St. John had a paper bag in his desk. She wasn't sure what to do with it if she found one, but she knew paper bags and hiccups went together like peanut butter and jelly. If she found a little one she'd blow into it, and if she found a big one she'd put it over her head. But then she wouldn't be able to drink her cognac.

The paper-bag dilemma took on gargantuan proportions as she riffled through the desk. It even took precedence over the less-immediate Mitch Summers dilemma. One thing at a time, she told herself, amazed at how methodically she was solving her problems. She blew her nose, wiped her tears, and poured herself another shot before tackling the file drawers in her search. Moving through *M,N,O, and P,* she didn't hear the key turn in the lock or the door open.

"What the hell?" That she heard.

"St. John," she cried, inordinately glad to see him. "Oh, St. John, I'm in trouble."

"You can say that again. What are you doing?" The question came out on a disbelieving sigh.

Anna returned her gaze to the files. "I'm looking, looking, you see, for a paper bag, and I'm almost to the *P's,* and—" Her head snapped up as another man walked into the room behind St. John.

"Mitch." She sighed, a weak smile lifting the corners of her mouth. "Oh, Mitch. I've been looking everywhere for you."

"I'm under *M.* I think you already passed me by." He gave her a crooked smile, but his eyes were troubled.

Anna suddenly wished she hadn't drunk quite as much cognac. She had so much to tell him, and her brain wouldn't connect with her mouth the right way. "Oh, Mitch." She tried to come up with something new to say, but "Oh, Mitch" was the best she could do, so she said it again. "Oh, Mitch."

"Oh, Anna. Oh, Anna." He actually chuckled as

he walked around the desk to help her in her attempt to stand up.

She wrapped her arms around his waist and snuggled her head under his chin. "I love you, Mitch. I love you, love you. Let's go to Hong Kong. We never got there before, remember?"

"I remember," he said, patting her on the shoulder.

Why didn't he hold her? She wanted so badly to be held. "Can we go there?" she asked, trying not to make too much of the stiffness of his body.

"You're drunk, Anna."

"I know. I'm terribly sorry. It's just that when I couldn't find you—"

"It's okay. Your brother and I have some business to take care of now. We'll talk later, when you know what you're saying." He set her aside and looked at St. John.

"Right." St. John helped her to a chair and made a quick phone call. Then he knelt in front of the safe, and Anna watched as he pulled out a sheaf of papers. A feeling of dread made her heart sink as he handed them to Mitch. They were the deeds to the ranch. Mitch hadn't come for her.

She needed to think, to sort this thing out. The harder she tried to focus her thoughts the more addled they became, until a knock sounded on the door and a shot of alarm cleared her brain for an instant.

St. John opened the door. Joe, his head bartender, was standing on the other side. "Would you please take Ms. Lange home?" St. John said. "We'll check the liquor order when you get back."

"Yes, sir, Mr. Lange." The bartender turned to Anna and offered his arm. "Ms. Lange?"

She pushed herself deeper into the chair and

grasped both arms. "I don't want to go home, St. John. I want to stay with Mitch," she mumbled, knowing she sounded absurd and that she wasn't in any condition to change matters. Why, oh, why, had she drunk so much?

"Go home, Anna," Mitch said. "I'll see you later."

Faced with his implacable stance, she reluctantly took the bartender's arm, but not before asking, "Promise?"

"Promise," he replied. His slight smile failed to warm her heart or increase her confidence.

The drive home was a blur of confusion. Mitch's actions signaled a loss of love Anna refused to accept. She must have misunderstood, but they could talk it all out this evening. Everything would work out for the best. She just had to believe in Mitch, in love. And she had to sober up.

Sobering up proved to be the biggest challenge she'd faced all day. Hot coffee and a cold shower woke her up, but failed to erase the muddle surrounding her mind. Her day was going from bad to worse, because with clarity came the undeniable conviction that she'd made a complete and total fool of herself. Mitch hadn't fallen in love with a fool, but he might have fallen out of love with one.

She needed to whip herself into shape. Hair, nails, facial, the works. Like a general preparing for battle, she swallowed a couple of aspirins and faced her less-than-glamorous reflection in the bathroom mirror. Buck up, baby. You can do it, she told herself with more conviction than she actually felt. She opened her bag of tricks and started laying her weapons on the counter. What Mother Nature couldn't fix with the time she had left Anna would either gloss over, cover up, or shade into being.

A hot bath and shampoo later, she began the real job of putting together the Anna Lange recognized around the world, the knock-your-socks-off Anna Lange.

Dusk had softened the ocean view from her bedroom window by the time she slipped into the midnight-blue satin gown. The dress was another carefully calculated move. Smiling, she remembered the effect it had had on Mitch the first night she'd met him, and she needed every ace she could get her hands on now. She zipped it up in back, then smoothed the gown over her hips, tucking each fold into place. All dressed up and no place to go, she thought, finally allowing herself to worry about Mitch's failure to call.

She spent a nervous fifteen minutes pacing the house before deciding to take matters in hand. As she'd figured, Mitch had checked into the Colonial, but he wasn't in his room. She paced for another fifteen minutes, then grabbed her purse and headed for Runner's Cay. Waiting time was over, and if he'd run out on her he was in for a big surprise, because she'd be on the next plane to Denver. Mitch Summers wouldn't go down in her memory as the one she let get away.

Anna left her car with the valet and breezed into the casino with a look that said she didn't have a care in the world. False bravado had carried her through many a sticky situation before, and she didn't hesitate to use it this time. Shoulders straight, head back, she walked confidently across the tiled foyer into the gambling rooms.

As she neared the bar, she saw him. Sitting

on the last stool in front of the open french doors, shoulders slumped, both arms resting on the bar, his hands loosely holding a highball glass, was Mitch. Her heart did a flip and her stomach tightened. He was wearing the worn tuxedo that set him apart from all the other well-dressed players, adding to the air of lonely dejection emanating from him.

She approached him cautiously, wanting to say the right words, to lift his spirits and touch his heart with her first move. The importance of their meeting slowed her steps even more. Her gaze roamed over his lean profile and the sandy-brown hair brushing against the winged and frayed collar of his shirt.

Standing silently beside him, she waited until he cocked his head and caught sight of her out of the corner of his eye. She smiled, a little sadly, then reached out and trailed her fingers down the side of his face and around the back of his neck. She pulled him closer until their lips met in the sweetest of kisses. Slowly he turned on his barstool, bringing her between his legs and wrapping his hands around her waist. The kiss deepened in drawn-out stages as they lingered on each nuance of rediscovery. Both of her hands tangled in his hair, caressing its silky texture.

Finally he lifted his head and searched her face with the eyes she longed to gaze into for the rest of her life. Soft eyes, eyes that didn't hide behind inherent mistrust.

"Why did you leave me?" he asked. His hands tightened around her waist, letting her know he wouldn't let her go this time.

She could have let him off easily, could have concocted a story he would have bought, but she wanted honesty, however painful. "Because you lied," she answered.

He nodded once, admitting his mistake without explanation. "Why did you come to find me tonight?"

"Because I love you," she said simply. Then she brushed her thumb along his cheek. "Why did you come back to Nassau?"

His gaze shifted from her eyes, and an arrow of fear shot straight down her insides. She had left herself wide open, laid her cards on the table, and it was too late to pull back.

He sighed and ran his hand through his hair. The silence lasted an eternity before he spoke. "I spent three days in the mountains after you left. Three days of proving to myself I could live without you. And . . ." He shook his head slowly from side to side. "I almost did it, Anna. Almost figured out a way to make the pain of losing you bearable."

Her heart pounded heavily in her chest, a lump hardened in her throat, and she felt as if her whole world hung on the meaning of *almost*.

He raised his head, and the bleakness of his memories was etched in the depths of his eyes. "You broke my heart, lady. And to top it off, your brother still had the deeds to my ranch. That's when I got mad, mad at myself for being a fool, mad at you for throwing away what we had."

"I'm sorry, Mitch," she whispered, her own heart breaking as she started to step away. She had lost, and she had to get out of there before she dissolved in tears.

But Mitch tightened his hold, one hand pressing her close, the other trailing up to her neck and bringing her head to his. She felt a lone tear track along her face from behind her tightly closed eyes. He caught it with his mouth and softly brushed his lips up to her ear.

"I love you, Anna." His voice was a husky breath. "And even the pain and the anger weren't enough to keep me away. When I saw you in St. John's office, my gut twisted with wanting you, wanting to hold you . . . love you . . . just talk to you."

His mouth was doing crazy things to the nape of her neck and she never wanted it to end, but even in her relief the tears kept flowing. Somehow this man had broken down all her barriers, pulled out all her emotional stops, leaving her vulnerable and ready for his love.

His mouth came back to her lips, branding her with a kiss. "Let's get out of here."

With his arm wrapped securely around her waist, he led her out the French doors to the veranda. In the dark quiet of the Bahamian night he backed her into the privacy of a lonely corner and unleashed the aching passion smoldering between them. He kissed her with an intensity that stopped her tears and left only thoughts of making love filling her mind.

His tongue flicked across her mouth, teasing and playing, drawing her desire to the surface. His breath became more ragged with each tender foray, his muscles tightening every place she touched him—and touch she did, every angle, every sweet, sensual region she remembered.

"Anna . . ." His voice caught as she ran her hand beneath his shirt. "We . . . uh, need to go someplace."

"I've got the key to a suite on the third floor," she whispered against his neck.

"Elevator?"

"Back stairs."

"Let's go."

When the door of the suite shut behind them, Mitch pulled her into his arms and hugged her, wrapping her in his warmth and love. Then a soft chuckle tickled her bare shoulder as he nuzzled her tawny skin.

"Ah, Anna. A great mystery is about to unfold. What *is* holding up this dress?"

"I think I'll let you figure that one out for yourself, scout." She kicked off her heels and drew him toward the bedroom, a smile curving her lips.

Later, when the moon was high and a silvery stream of light played shadows across the bed, Mitch propped himself up on the pillows and took her hand in his. He entwined their fingers, then raised their hands to his mouth and opened the palms. A soft kiss close to her thumb preceded his words.

"I don't know how we're going to pull this off, Anna, but I'm going to give it everything I've got. Which isn't much. Which is most of the problem."

Her brow furrowed, and she pulled up the sheet and tucked it under her arms. "What are you talking about, Mitch?"

"Money. Lifestyles. St. John told me about Antonio. Must have been rough, huh?"

"It was a long time ago, Mitch," she said, and finally it did seem like a long time ago. The weight of an ancient grudge had begun to dissipate after the reconciliation with her father, and Mitch's love had dispelled the last of her burden. But she wasn't at all sure of the direction this conversation was taking.

"After you left the office today," Mitch continued, "your big brother took the opportunity to set me straight on a few things. He told me you were slumming with me. That I was some kind of quirky diversion for a rich girl who could do a lot better with someone in her own class. I can't change what I am, Anna. A million dollars isn't going to fall out of the sky into my bank account."

"Well, scout." She relaxed back into the pillows and gave the impression of seriously contemplating his words, but she didn't let go of his hand. "That might be for the best. I mean, look at it this way. If the million came down as gold it would probably wipe out the whole lobby, and if it came down in bills it'd probably all get lost on the wind or something. Besides, we've already got a million, give or take a few hundred thousand on any day of the week. And we've got the ranch"—she cocked a delicately arched brow and smiled slyly— "and we've got the Speedster."

"Anna, I'm trying to be serious."

"You're not going to let me drive the Speedster?"

"Of course you can drive the Speedster, but—"

"Can you have me on two-hundreds by Christmas?"

"*Next* Christmas, maybe. If you really work at it."

"This Christmas, next Christmas." She shrugged and nonchalantly flicked her hand. "Christmas twenty years from now. We can take all the time we need."

He shot her a wary glance. Then a slow grin widened his mouth in the funny way that fought with his nose, endearing him to her heart. "Are you trying to tell me something?"

"You catch on fast, boy scout. How long does ski season last?"

"Five months, give or take a week at either end of the season."

"Half a year there, half a year here. What do you think?"

"I think there's an awful lot of giving and taking going on here."

She laid his hand on her hip and snuggled closer under the sheets. With a gentle sigh she whispered, "Isn't that the way it's supposed to be in a marriage."

His body stiffened for an instant, and then, just as quickly, he rolled over on top of her, trapping her beneath his weight. "You *are* trying to tell me something."

A cloud floated over the moon, taking the stream of light from the room, but Anna felt the smile in his voice and the love shining in his eyes. The brush of his thumbs tracing the contours of her face filled her with a happiness sweeter than any she'd ever known. It was always that way with Mitch's touching. It went beyond the physical, communicating to her on a level she hadn't known existed, until he came into her world.

He lowered his head, and his mouth moved across hers, lightly, lovingly. "Will you marry me, Anna?" he asked between kisses.

"Tomorrow . . . tonight . . . yesterday." She savored each meeting of their lips. "The answer is yes."

"I don't believe in long engagements," he said warningly.

"Next week. Miami. We'll keep it small, but I want my father to give me away. Do you want your family there?"

"I'll fly my mom out, but the rest of them are on their own. We can have a reception in San Francisco after the honeymoon. Let's go to Eleuthera, Robby's place, okay?"

She brushed a swath of hair off his forehead, letting her fingers linger while she thought over his words. "You're a very nice man, Mitch. I know it will mean a lot to Robby to have us come to Sandy Bay. He's a good friend. Thanks for thinking of him." She let her hand trail down his face and brushed her thumb over his mouth, knowing there was one more thing she had to give him to prove their love would last a lifetime. "When do you have to be back at work?" she asked.

He didn't answer at first, taking time to steal another kiss. Then, with his mouth still on hers, she felt his laughter shake them and the bed. "You're really going to be mine," he said. "*You* are really going to be mine."

"I've been yours since you kissed my hand," she admitted, her own laughter bubbling up to meet his.

"I knew it, Anna, but I was beginning to wonder if I could convince you."

"Believe me, scout, I'm convinced." And she was. He was a special man who made her feel like a special woman, cherished for reasons other than her looks and money. He had seen something in her that no one else ever had, and that knowledge had set her free and opened her heart. "So when do we go home?"

"Home." He drew the word out in a long sigh. "After my ring is on your finger, after we make love in the ocean"—his body moved against hers— "after we make love on the beach in the moonlight, then we'll go home."

She pulled his mouth down to hers for a brief kiss filled with all the love in her heart. "Ah, yes, Mitch. Then we'll go home."

THE EDITOR'S CORNER

We have some wonderful news for you this month. Beginning with our October 1987 books, LOVESWEPT will be publishing *six* romances a month, not just four! We are very excited about this, and we hope all of you will be just as thrilled. Many of you have asked, requested, even pleaded with us over the years to publish more than four books a month, but we have always said that we wouldn't unless we were certain the quality of the books wouldn't suffer. We are confident now that, with all of the wonderful authors who write such fabulous books for us and all the new authors we are discovering, our future books will be just as much fun and just as heartwarming and beloved as those we've already published. And to let you know what you have to look forward to, I'll give you the titles and authors of the books we will be publishing in October 1987 (on sale in September).

#210 KISMET
by Helen Mittermeyer

#211 EVENINGS IN PARIS
by Kathleen Downes

#212 BANISH THE DRAGONS
by Margie McDonnell

#213 LEPRECHAUN
by Joan Elliott Pickart

#214 A KNIGHT TO REMEMBER
by Olivia and Ken Harper

#215 LOVING JENNY
by Billie Green

Before I go on to tell you about the delightful LOVESWEPTs in store for you next month, I want to remind you that Nora Roberts's romantic suspense novel, **HOT ICE,** is on sale right now. As I mentioned last month, it's dynamite, filled with intrigue, danger, exotic locations, and—of course!—features a fabulous hero and a fabulous heroine whom I know you will love. He's a professional thief; she's a reckless heiress looking for excitement. When he jumps into her Mercedes at a stoplight and a high-speed chase ensues, both Doug Lord and Whitney MacAllister get more than they bargained for! I'm sure you will love **HOT ICE,** so do get your copy now!

We start off our August LOVESWEPTs with Patt Bucheister,

(continued)

who has given us another tender and warm story in **TOUCH THE STARS,** LOVESWEPT #202. Diana Dragas can't stand reporters because they destroyed her father's career as a diplomat. This causes problems for the handsome and virile Michael Dare, who is captivated by the beautiful Diana—and is, alas, also a reporter. Still, Diana can't resist this gallant charmer and allows Michael to sweep her away. When she discovers he's misled her, she has to make the most important decision of her life. As always, Patt has created two wonderful people whom we can truly care about.

Peggy Webb's newest LOVESWEPT, **SUMMER JAZZ,** #203, is as hot and sultry as the title suggests. Mattie Houston comes home from Paris looking for sweet revenge on Hunter Chadwick, the impossibly handsome man who'd broken her heart years earlier. Both Mattie and Hunter are certain their love has died, but neither has forgotten that summer of sunshine and haunting jazz when they'd fallen shamelessly in love—and it takes only one touch for that love to be resurrected. But all the misunderstandings and pain of the past must be put to rest before they can be free to love again. This is a powerful, moving story that I'm sure you'll remember for a long time.

Joan Elliott Pickart has always been well loved for her humor, and **REFORMING FREDDY,** LOVESWEPT #204, has an opening that is as unique as it is funny. Tricia Todd never imagined that her physical fitness program—walking up the four flights of stairs to her office—could be so dangerous! Halfway up, she's confronted by a young thief, and she shocks herself as much as the teenager by whipping out her nephew's water pistol. She threatens to shoot Freddy, the young criminal, and gets more than her man—she gets two men. Lt. Spence Walker, rugged, handsome, and cynical, is certain that Tricia, a bright-eyed optimist, is all wrong for him. So why can't he keep away from her? And furthermore, what is she doing when she's mysteriously out of her office at odd hours during the day? Actually, Tricia is doing exactly what Spence told her not to do—reforming Freddy. You'll laugh out loud as Tricia tries to deal with both Freddy and

(continued)

Spence, teaching each—in very different ways—that they don't have to be afraid of love.

Next, Susan Richardson's **A SLOW SIMMER**, LOVE-SWEPT #205, pairs two unlikely people—gourmet cook Betsy Carmody and hunk-of-any-month quarterback Jesse Kincaid. Betsy and Jesse had known each other years earlier, when Betsy was married to another player on the San Francisco football team. That marriage was a disaster, and she wants to have nothing to do with the big, mischievous, and handsome Jesse . . . but he doesn't believe in taking no for an answer and just keeps coming back, weakening her resistance with his sexy smiles and heart-stopping kisses. This is a charming love story, and Jesse is a hero you'll cheer for, both on and off the field.

Do I need to remind you that the next three books of the Delaney Dynasty go on sale next month? If you haven't already asked your bookseller to reserve copies for you, be sure to do so now. The trilogy has the overall title **THE DELANEYS OF KILLAROO,** and the individual book titles are:

Adelaide, The Enchantress
by Kay Hooper

Matilda, The Adventuress
by Iris Johansen

Sydney, The Temptress
by Fayrene Preston

Enjoy!

Sincerely,

Carolyn Nichols

Carolyn Nichols
  Editor
LOVESWEPT
Bantam Books, Inc.
666 Fifth Avenue
New York, NY 10103

It's a little like being Loveswept

SHEER MADNESS

SHEER COLOR

SHEER PASSION

SHEER EXCITEMENT

SHEER INTRIGUE

SHEER ROMANCE

All it takes is a little imagination and more Pazazz.®

Coming this July from Clairol…Pazazz Sheer Color Wash
—8 inspiring sheer washes of color that last up to 4 shampoos.

Look for the Free Loveswept *THE DELANEYS OF KILLAROO* book sampler this July in participating stores carrying Pazazz Sheer Color Wash.